Movie Novelization

Adapted by Ellen Miles from the screenplay
by Alfred Gough & Miles Millar

SCHOLASTIC INC.
New York   Toronto   London   Auckland   Sydney
Mexico City   New Delhi   Hong Kong   Buenos Aires

ISBN 0-439-47256-3

12 11 10 9 8 7 6 5 4 3 2   3 4 5 6 7 8/0

Printed in the U.S.A.
First printing, February 2003

CHAPTER ONE:
The Forbidden City

One soft, fat snowflake drifted down out of a blank white sky. It fell slowly, lazily, until it landed without a sound on the very top of the Gate of Supreme Harmony. Then another snowflake fell, and another, until there were dozens of them, huge white flakes dancing in the sky over the smooth red-tiled roofs.

It was a winter day in 1887, and snow was blanketing the Forbidden City of China. It fell on the roof of the Hall of Celestial Purity, and piled up on the Pavilion of Cheerful

Melodies. It covered the golden lion sculptures in the courtyard, and outlined the paths leading to each one of the Six East Palaces and the Six West Palaces.

It grew dark, and still the snow fell. A beautiful young woman with porcelain skin stepped through a circular entrance and hurried through the courtyard of the Imperial Palace, carrying a glowing lantern of scarlet silk in one hand and a teapot in the other. The massive vermillion walls of the palace loomed above her small frame as she crossed over a marble bridge, her robes sweeping the snow aside. She approached the steps that led to a pair of gigantic red wooden doors. A pair of Imperial Guards stiffened, then relaxed when they saw the familiar face.

At the top of the stairs, another pair of guards stood watch over the doors. The young woman held up her teapot. The guards smiled and moved to open the enormous doors, which creaked as they yawned wide. The woman slipped through the doors and clicked along the corridors until she arrived in the Dragon Pavilion.

Inside, pennants of brightly colored silk

covered with images of writhing turquoise dragons drifted from the ceiling. The woman tiptoed across the glassy floor and peered through a lattice screen. Her tiny gasp echoed throughout the quiet room.

The old man behind the screen turned to see her. "Chon Lin," he admonished her. "You are not permitted to gaze at the Imperial Seal. How often must I tell you?" He was kneeling in front of a gold chest, wiping a silk cloth over the Seal as if to polish the already gleaming gold. The fist-sized diamond that crowned the Seal twinkled in the dim light. Chon Lin caught only a glimpse of its magnificence before her father whisked the Seal back into its chest. He locked the door with the dragon key that hung around his neck.

"Sorry, Father," whispered Chon Lin.

The old man stood up and smiled at his daughter. "Come," he said. "The tea is getting cold."

Outside, in the courtyard, an Imperial Guard patrolled the grounds. Suddenly, he stopped and held himself very still, listening hard. Then he began to walk again, over the

*marble bridge and through the circular en-
trance. Just as he stepped into the circle, a
length of rope looped around his neck and
whisked him off his feet.*

Chon Lin and her father sat on the floor
behind a folding screen, sipping their tea.
Neither of them spoke. Looking across the
low table between them, Chon Lin studied
her father's face. Slowly, hesitatingly, she
pulled something from her pocket. She cleared
her throat. "I received a letter from Chon
Wang," she said softly.

The old man looked up in surprise. The familiar name seemed to hang in the air between them.

Chon Lin did not meet his eyes. Instead,
she slid a photograph across the table. In
soft tones of sepia, it showed a handsome
Chinese man wearing the clothing of the
American West. A sheriff's star shone from
his chest. Next to him was a brown-and-
white horse that sat in the posture of a dog.

The old man barely glanced at the picture.
His face was twisted with bitterness and regret.

"He is doing well in America," Chon Lin told her father. "He sends his love."

The old man snatched up the photo. "Your brother is dead to me, Chon Lin," he said, as he held it over the candle flame.

Outside, two massive bronze lions stared at the guards at the base of the steps. All was quiet. Then, with a sudden swishing noise, two arrows darted through the swirling snow. The guards fell without a sound. At the top of the steps, the guards at the door turned to see two hulking Chinese men dressed in black. Their red turbans glowed through the falling snow. So did the gleaming curved blades of their swords.

Boxers.

Members of a secret society, also known as The Righteous and Harmonious Fists, they practiced a secret, deadly form of martial arts. Their goal? A bloody rebellion that would drive all foreigners from China.

Before the guards could fight them off, the Boxers cut them down with a flurry of quick, lethal strokes. Then a third Boxer appeared from the shadows, accompanied by a tall, blond Englishman. All four stormed inside the Imperial Palace, heading straight for the Chamber of the Imperial Seal.

Nelson Rathbone, dashing as always, strode confidently towards the golden chest that held the Seal. He was half a step away when the blade of a sword swung up, wavering, only millimeters from his neck.

"Not one step further, foreign devil!" said the old man.

Rathbone raised an eyebrow. "Ah," he said, "the Keeper of the Imperial Seal."

One of the Boxers raised his crossbow, but before he could aim it was kicked out of his hands.

Rathbone turned to Chon Lin, who had placed the kick, and smiled a thin, humorless smile. "A woman," he noted. "You Chinese are very progressive."

Chon Lin's father frowned. "Chon Lin," he said urgently. "Get help."

"That won't be necessary," drawled Rathbone, as the Boxers launched themselves at Chon Lin. She dodged their blades, landing blows of her own as she lashed out with hands and feet. As she fought the three men, Rathbone pulled a dagger from his sleeve. It was a beautiful weapon, carved in the form of a coiled dragon, with gleaming red rubies for eyes. Without a pause, he thrust it into the old man's chest. "A gift," he said, "from an old friend."

The old man looked surprised at first. Then he understood. "Wu Yip," he said, with the last bit of energy left in his body.

Rathbone nodded. "He wanted me to send his regards," he said, as the old man slumped to the floor. Rathbone reached for the dragon key and pulled it free from the old man's neck. Ignoring the battle still raging behind him, he stepped to the golden chest, unlocked it, and lifted out the treasure he had come to steal. For a moment, as he gazed upon the Seal, Nelson Rathbone's face lost its customary superior sneer.

Behind him, one of the Boxers swept a sword at Chon Lin. She leapt into the air and the sword embedded itself in a column behind her. As the other Boxers rushed toward her, she leapt onto the sword's blade and springboarded up into a somersault high over their heads, sweeping her foot into Rathbone's face as he turned to look.

Rathbone fell backwards, crashing into the golden chest. A red line of blood appeared on his cheekbone and his cold, gray eyes flashed with anger. He jumped to his feet to face a furious Chon Lin. The Boxers circled nearby, awaiting orders, but Rathbone, who heard the sound of Imperial Guards approaching, preferred to finish the job himself. With a lightning-fast kick to her chest he sent Chon Lin flying back into a screen. Rathbone grabbed the Seal, motioned to the Boxers, and disappeared.

Chon Lin struggled to her feet. She was about to run after the villains when she heard her father moan. She rushed to his side. "Father!" she whispered, peering into his dying eyes.

"The Seal . . ." he moaned. "You must get it back . . . promise me!"

Chon Lin's eyes filled with tears — and determination. "I promise," she vowed.

Her father gazed up at her. Then, with tremendous effort, he reached into the pocket of his robes and pulled out a small box carved out of ivory. "Give . . . give this to your brother," he gasped. With that, his eyes closed and his head fell back.

Chon Lin closed her own eyes and said a silent prayer. Then she took a deep breath and stood up, her shoulders squared and her head held high. She left the Dragon Pavilion without looking back, walking softly across the cold, smooth floor.

CHAPTER TWO:
Carson City

Some weeks later, in America . . .
Inside the Carson City jailhouse, Sheriff Chon Wang stamped "Arrested" across the pictures of various desperadoes as his deputy leaned back in his chair reading a book. A gallery of similar pictures papered the walls, a testament to the talents of the local law.

"What are you reading?" Wang asked his partner.

"Roy O' Bannon Versus the Mummy," replied the deputy, showing Wang the comic-book-

style cover of his dime novel. "It's incredible. Roy's just taken out the Mummy's army of zombie confederate soldiers — and he only had one bullet!"

Wang shook his head. "That is not possible," he remarked.

"Yeah, it is," said the deputy, sitting up to explain. "See, Roy figured out the physics of the canyon, then ricocheted the bullet and nailed each zombie through the heart."

"What about the Shanghai Kid?" Wang asked casually.

"He was captured and knocked out on page ten," explained the deputy, "while he was polishing Roy's pearlhandles. But don't worry, Roy's about to save him from becoming a human sacrifice."

Wang shook his head. "Those stories are all lies," he said.

"No, they're not!" insisted the deputy. "It says so right here on the back." He turned the book over and read, "Author Sage McAllister bases his stories on firsthand accounts." He pointed to a picture of a man with wild white hair and a bushy mustache. He sighed. "It must have been something riding with a true-blue Western hero like Roy O' Bannon," he said.

"Sometimes I find it hard to believe myself," Wang answered drily. Then, hearing a stagecoach rattle by outside, he grabbed his hat and ran out the door. He raced down the dusty boardwalk, spit-shining his badge as he drew near the stage.

"Sorry, Sheriff," said the driver. "No princess."

Wang bowed his head, disappointed. His deputy caught up just then. "Every day you meet the noon stage," he told his boss, "and every day it's the same story. She's not coming back."

Wang shrugged. "Pei Pei is married to her work in San Francisco," he said sadly. "Modern women."

Just then, the driver handed Wang a package. "Parcel for you, Sheriff."

The deputy peered at the address. "Fancy Chinese writing," he commented. "Maybe it's from her."

"No," said Wang. "It is from my sister in China." He tore open the parcel to find an intricately carved ivory box — and a letter. His face grew stiff and sad as he read his sister's words.

Twenty-four hours later, Wang walked out of the jailhouse with his saddlebag over his shoulder. He approached a brown-and-white horse that sat in the posture of a dog. "Fido," he said, "I must go. You stay here and be a good horsey for the new sheriff." Fido licked his master's face as Wang took off his star and pinned it to his deputy's chest. Then Wang walked toward a waiting stagecoach.

"That stage is headed east," said the deputy. "Isn't China kinda west of here?"

"I am not going to China," replied Wang. "I am going to New York. Roy has invested my money. He says he is building me a nest egg."

The deputy looked impressed. "Is it true that he lives in a penthouse at the Waldorf Astoria, with fancy food and dozens of beautiful women wanting to marry him?"

Wang shook his head. "That is the old Roy," he said. "He has settled down. Trust me, he has changed."

CHAPTER THREE:
Roy at the Waldorf

Roy O'Bannon gazed at the rapt faces staring up at him and went on with the story he'd been telling. "So, there we were," he said, "completely outnumbered. I knew we didn't have a chance, so I sent the Shanghai Kid and the Princess out the back. Then I counted to three and burst out of the mission with my pearlhandles burning." He paused to let them imagine the scene. "And not one bullet touched me," he finished.

"What happened to the emperor's gold?" asked a girl in the audience.

"We divided it up," Roy told her. "But I insisted on giving my share to the Indians."

Suddenly, someone shouted behind him.

"Reach for the sky, Roy!"

Roy let out a wild screech and ducked behind a little old lady. He spun her around and found himself staring into the face of his old partner. "John!" he cried. "You almost scared this old woman to death." He turned the woman to face him. "Are you all right, ma'am?"

The woman tottered away as Roy wrapped Wang in a huge hug. The Shanghai Kid couldn't have looked any more out of place in his Western gear: chaps, hat, and all, with a dusty old pair of saddlebags slung over one shoulder. "John Wayne!" cried Roy. "What brings you to New York?"

Wang met his eyes. "My share of the gold," he said flatly.

Roy looked at him. "John, we've known each other a long time. Stop beating around the bush. If you want something, just come out and say it."

"I want my share of the gold," Wang repeated patiently.

Roy frowned as if trying to recall. "Refresh my memory, John. What gold are we talking about?"

"The emperor's gold," Wang answered, sounding a little less patient.

"Oh, *that* gold!" Roy smiled nervously. "See, it's in what the Wall Street pros call a 'long-term investment.'"

"I need it tonight," said Wang. He did not return Roy's smile.

"What's the rush?" asked Roy. "You only just got here. Let me introduce you to some friends."

Wang ignored him. "I need the money. My father has been killed."

Roy's eyes widened. His nervous chatter stopped. "John," he said seriously. "I'm real sorry to hear that. Do you need the money to get home for his funeral?"

Wang shook his head. "No. I need it to get to England to avenge his murder. The ship leaves tonight."

"Wait," said a baffled Roy, holding up a hand. "Your father was killed in England?"

Wang shook his head again. "No. China. My sister, she followed the murderer to London."

Roy looked more confused than ever. "Whoa, John, slow down. Information overload. Let's get the pertinent facts straight." He thought for a second. "You have a sister?" he asked, as if it were the only piece of information he'd digested. "How come you never told me about her? Is she cute — or does she look like you?"

"Roy," Wang said, still unsmiling, "I need my money."

Roy winced. "Hey, John, I don't appreciate that tone. You really think I'd stiff you, after all we've been through?" He waved around as if to show off his surroundings. "In case you hadn't noticed, I'm doing pretty well."

Wang nodded. "Sorry, Roy," he said.

"It's okay," Roy said generously. "I know you're under a lot of pressure, but you've got to be more trusting —"

Just then, the Waldorf's headwaiter tapped Roy on the shoulder. "O' Bannon," he said. "The couple at table five is ready to order."

Surprised, Wang looked at Roy. "Do you work here?"

"No, no," Roy insisted. "He was confused. I just happen to have the same jacket as the waiting staff."

"How did he know your name?" Wang asked.

Roy shrugged. "I'm a regular. I'm here all the time."

Just then, another waiter passed by, handing Roy a wad of folded bills. "Roy, here's your cut of the tips," he said.

Roy blushed as he accepted the money. "I'm telling you," he told Wang. "It's the craziest thing."

Wang just folded his arms and looked at his old friend.

"You lost the gold playing poker," he guessed.

Roy was cornered, and he knew it. "Not all of it," he said in a tiny voice.

"Then where's the rest?" Wang didn't really have to ask. He could see the answer in Roy's face. Horse racing, dinners at fine restaurants, nights at the theater . . . Roy had been living it up, on their money.

Roy started babbling, something about investing in zeppelins, but Wang interrupted him. "Roy, I need my money now. I must leave tonight!"

Roy thought for a second. "Maybe we can get it from some of my fans," he said. "Let me work on it." He went back to his audience.

A couple of hours later, Roy burst into John's room. "John, we've got trouble!"

It turned out that one of the people Roy had tried to con was the mayor! Now he'd come back to the hotel with a crew of cops, and they were looking for Roy.

"I see you have not changed," Wang said, shaking his head at his friend's ways.

Roy hung his head. "I know. I want to, John, I really do."

"So, now what's the plan?" asked Wang.

"I guess I need to settle down . . ." Roy began.

Wang grabbed him by the lapels and shook him. "No, Roy, the plan is to get out of here!"

"Oh," said Roy. "This way." He led Wang toward the elevator. "Watch out for those cops," Roy warned, as they headed for the revolving door.

Wang looked around. The coast was clear. He pushed into the revolving door — just in time to see the two cops waiting outside. Wang let the door rotate past them, but they stepped into the compartment of the door right behind his!

Wang jumped out into the lobby.

The cops jumped out after him, swinging their nightsticks.

Wang leapt and ducked to avoid their blows, then slipped back into the door as it revolved back into the street. He reached out to grab a cane from an old man walking by, let the door swing him around again, and took out the two cops with a few quick blows. Just then, two more cops jumped into his space as the door kept revolving.

Finally, Wang stepped out of the door and onto the street, two unconscious policemen tumbling out ahead of him. Calmly, he handed the cane back to the stunned old man.

Roy was watching the whole thing from behind a bellman's cart full of suitcases and trunks. "Psst," he called to his friend. "This way," he said. "I've got our ticket out of here."

CHAPTER FOUR:
Wang and Roy at Sea

The huge ocean liner pulled away from the pier, blowing a long, loud blast of farewell. Deep inside the hold was an enormous trunk, plastered with stickers that read "London, England."

"Hear that?" said a voice from inside the trunk. "We're on our way to England. You didn't think I could do it, but your buddy Roy came through again."

Suddenly, the lid of the trunk flew open. An angry-looking Wang popped out, looking down at his friend. "Yes," he said. "Just like old times."

Roy stretched. "John," he said, "I'm sorry about that gold, but you'll be thanking me when that first zeppelin takes off." Wang wasn't listening. He walked through the door as Roy went on. "Hey, you're lucky I didn't invest in that ridiculous horseless carriage scheme!"

Later, Roy found Wang leaning against the railing as the ship glided past the twinkling lights of the New York City skyline. Wang held a small, intricately carved box in his hands. "John," Roy said, "I'm sorry I lied to you. I just didn't want you to be disappointed in me."

Wang just looked at him.

"See, that's what I mean," Roy said. "That look. I can't take it!"

Wang looked down at the box in his hand. He was trying to open it, but getting nowhere. "I learned it from my father," he said softly. "That is how he used to look at me."

Roy was interested. "Was he an Imperial Guard?"

"No," Wang told him. "Much more important. He was Keeper of the Imperial Seal."

Roy grinned and smacked his hand on the railing. "That's what I love about China," he said. "Everybody's job description is so cool."

Wang told him more. "Since Genghis Khan the Seal has been the symbol of the emperor's power. My family has watched over it for twelve generations." He stared down at the waves far beneath them. "We used to skip stones across the moat and talk about the day I would follow in his foot-steps."

Roy nodded. "But then you came to America, and there went *that* plan."

Wang sighed. "I was his only son. If I had been there, I could have protected him. This is all my fault."

"You were three thousand miles away," Roy said. "You can't blame yourself." He watched Wang struggling with the box. "What's with the fancy little box?"

"My sister sent it to me," Wang answered. "It's a puzzle box. There's a message from my father inside."

"Why don't you just use a hammer to bash it open?" Roy asked.

Wang spoke softly. "I must have patience.

By the time I work out how to open it, I will be ready to read the message."

Roy nodded. "That's the corniest thing I ever heard," he said. "And the most beautiful." He took the box and looked at it. "You know, my heart is like this box," he mused. "I've never known how to open it, haven't had the patience. I need to find my key. Maybe this trip will help me figure it out." He handed the box back to his friend. "We'll get to London, catch your dad's killer, and get that seal back," he vowed.

Want looked at Roy. "There is no reward in this," he warned his friend. "The Seal must be returned to the Forbidden City."

"I'm not doing this for the reward," Roy answered, just as solemnly. "This is about friendship and loyalty and honor."

Wang looked into his eyes. "Thank you, Roy," he said.

The two friends turned to watch as the ship glided past the partially assembled Statue of Liberty, just barely lit up by the first rays of dawn.

"Plus," Roy added, "I hear England is full of beautiful girls."

CHAPTER FIVE:
Oh, My Lord

Meanwhile, inside London's most famous landmark, the Houses of Parliament, the lord chancellor hammered his gavel to silence the rowdy members of the House of Lords. In the sudden quiet, Big Ben, the giant clock that loomed high above Parliament, boomed out the hour. The lord chancellor smoothed his magnificent robes. "First order of business, my lords, is a report from our esteemed friend, Lord Rathbone, who recently returned from a diplomatic mission to China."

The applause was weak. Rathbone rose to his feet, looking slightly peeved. The scar on his left cheek was still red, not yet fully healed. "Fellow lords," he began, "I am afraid I bring you disturbing news from the Orient. The Opium Wars have ravaged the land and the emperor's enemies are organizing. The most vicious are the Boxers, a godless band of rebels who murder without discretion. China is not well."

The lords murmured.

"I shall pass on your report to the prime minister," said the lord chancellor.

Rathbone bowed slightly in acknowledgement. "I have brought back an envoy who will give us insight into the inscrutable mind of the Chinese." He gestured to two footmen, who swung open the large doors. A keeper led a massive, snarling white Siberian tiger into the chamber. The lords gasped in delight. "The newest addition to the Regent's Park Zoo," Rathbone explained, "given to her Majesty Queen Victoria by the emperor, in recognition of her fifty glorious years on the throne." He paused for a moment, then added, "God save the queen."

Later, a satisfied Rathbone strode out of Parliament and climbed behind the wheel of a gleaming motorcar. Everyone on the street turned to stare at the newfangled machine. As Rathbone pulled into the street, he glanced into his mirror to see a thin, catlike Chinese man sitting behind him. The man held a cane tipped with the head of a dragon. "Wu Yip!" Rathbone exclaimed. "Do you have any notion of what would happen if we were seen together?"

Wu Yip's face was impassive. "Since your return," he said, "I have yet to lay eyes on the Imperial Seal." His English was impeccable.

Rathbone's lips tightened. "The queen's Jubilee is in four days," he said. "You'll get the Seal once you have completed your end of the arrangement."

Wu Yip's eyes flashed. "Do you have so little faith in me?" he asked. "Royal blood runs in my veins, too."

"There's nothing royal about you, Wu Yip," Rathbone sneered.

"I may only be the emperor's half brother," Wu Yip replied, drawing himself up, "but I am the rightful heir to the Chinese throne."

Rathbone snorted. "You're a common criminal."

"I am also your partner," Wu Yip reminded him. "And I insist on seeing the Seal if our partnership is going to continue."

Rathbone heard the tone in his voice. He gave in. "I'm hosting a Jubilee ball at my country estate tomorrow. Be at the stables at midnight." He reached into a brocaded bag and pulled out a weapon: the cobra dagger he had used to murder the Keeper of the Imperial Seal. "As requested," he said, handing it to Wu Yip, "a token of my esteem."

Wu Yip gazed at the dried blood staining the blade. "He never should have betrayed me," he said softly.

Rathbone pulled the car over to the curb. "This is where you get out," he told his passenger.

Wu Yip opened the door. But before he stepped out, he turned to Rathbone. "I hope there will be more trust between us," he said, "when I am emperor and you are the new king of England."

CHAPTER SIX:
Howdy, London!

"Howdy, partner!" Wang said, tipping his cowboy hat to the people passing on the sidewalk. He and Roy had just stepped off a train and into the hustle and bustle of the London streets. They did not exactly blend in. Roy was still wearing his white dinner jacket, and Wang was in full sheriff gear, saddlebags and all. Top-hatted gentlemen and ladies in long skirts stared at them as they ambled down the sidewalk, glancing around to take in all the sights.

"The English do not seem friendly," Wang remarked.

"Don't worry about it," Roy assured him. "They're just sore losers." Without looking to his right, he stepped off a curb — and straight into the path of a horse-drawn double-decker bus. "Hey!" he shouted. "You're driving on the wrong side of the road, moron!"

"What did they lose?" asked Wang, as the two of them picked their way through the throngs of carriages and pedestrians filling the street.

"Only a little skirmish called the American Revolution," Roy answered.

"Never heard of it," admitted Wang, as the two men passed a group of giggling young women who seemed to find Wang's dusty clothing particularly funny.

Roy waved to the girls. "Ladies," he said, grinning at them. Then he caught the disapproving expression on Wang's face. "What?" he asked. "I'm not allowed to be friendly?"

"I thought you wanted to settle down and have a family," Wang reminded him.

"I do!" cried Roy. "I'm going to have a whole pack of kids. I love the little ankle-biters.

Oof!" He grunted as a young boy bumped into him, hard. Roy stared at the boy, who looked to be about ten years old. He wore a bowler hat, a ratty black jacket, and baggy pants full of holes and patches. "Hey, punk!" Roy said. "Watch where you're going."

The boy tipped his hat, a twinkle in his eye. "Pardon me, guv," he said. He looked the two men over. "The name's Charlie. You gents lost your way?"

Roy was about to shoo him off, but Wang pulled a letter out of his pocket. "We are looking for my sister," he told the boy. "She is staying at —" he checked the address on the letter, "Twenty-seven Broad Street."

Charlie nodded. "Know it well, guv," he said instantly. "My old man used to live there."

Wang looked hopeful. "Can you show us the way?"

Charlie thought for a moment. "My memory's a little dodgy," he said finally, "but I'm sure for five bob I could get you there."

At that, Roy shook his head in disgust. "The kid's trying to shake you down, John. He's going to take your money and lead you on a wild-goose chase." He turned to Charlie.

"I can't believe people still fall for that routine over here. You need a new trick, kid. That one's been done to death."

Charlie looked up at Roy, his eyes all innocent. Then, with a tiny smile, he held something up.

A gold pocket watch.

"Thanks for the tip, guv," he said. And he took off, dashing down a nearby alley.

Roy felt his pockets. "Hey! I stole that watch from my uncle!" he shouted. He and Wang took off after the boy, sprinting as fast as they could toward Covent Garden marketplace.

The area was a maze of pushcarts, loaded with fruit and vegetables. Flower girls strolled along, selling sweet-smelling bouquets of violets and roses. Seedy-looking characters lurked in every corner. Wang and Roy chased Charlie down the main aisle of the marketplace, arriving just in time to see the leader of a gang of pickpockets grab the boy and throw him against a wall.

"What did I tell you about poaching on our turf, Charlie?" asked the man dressed in rags. His thin face was hard and threatening.

"I'm on the straight and narrow, honest!" blurted Charlie.

The pickpocket frisked him and pulled out the pocket watch. "What's this, then?" he snarled. "After I'm through beating you, you're going to wish you never ran away from the workhouse."

The other pickpockets gathered around, eager for the show.

"Leave the boy alone." It was Wang, standing nearby with folded arms.

The leader turned with a sneer. "Tourists!" he said. "Keep your noses out of it."

Now Roy spoke up. "That's my watch you're holding," he told the man.

The pickpocket just laughed. "There's eight of us and two of you," he said. "So bug off."

Wham! Wang aimed a kick right at the lead pickpocket's stomach. As he fell, Charlie snatched the watch and took off. Roy chased after him — and so did the thieves.

Wang blocked their way.

Two of them pulled out knives, the blades gleaming. They came at Wang, waving their weapons.

Wang grabbed an oversized umbrella off a

nearby cart of melons. Closing it, he held the shaft like a fighting stick and whip-spun the knives right out of their hands! Then, to finish off the job, he used the end of the umbrella like a baseball bat to pound a couple of melons at the two men. They staggered backwards, right into a cart full of eggs. Dozens of them flew towards Wang.

He popped open the umbrella just in time. The sticky yellow goo oozed down the sides.

Another pickpocket charged Wang.

Wang thrust the umbrella at him, flipping him off his feet, high into the air. *Wham!* The villain crash-landed in a cart full of spiny pineapples.

Wang replaced the umbrella.

An instant later, he was rammed by a potato cart that sent him flying. He landed next to a flower girl. Grabbing her basket, he held it up just in time to catch the knives two other pickpockets thrust at him.

He smiled at the girl.

She smiled back, showing a row of blackened stumps.

Wang leapt to his feet and ran down the aisle, looking for Roy. He found him playing cat and mouse with Charlie around a line of stalls. Just as Wang arrived, the boy grabbed an apple from a cart, setting the rest of the fruit rolling in a massive avalanche that swept Roy right off his feet.

"Repent, the end is near!"

Wang turned to see a street preacher wearing a wooden sandwich board around his neck. The preacher walked towards them, shouting and ringing a bell.

At lightning speed, Wang ducked under the board and flipped it off the preacher and onto his own neck. As two more pickpockets approached, closing in quickly, Wang split-kicked the board up into their faces. Another thief came at him, roaring with anger. Wang grabbed the bell out of the preacher's hand and sent it spinning through the air until it smashed into the thief's head, sending him flying.

Wang flipped the board back onto the preacher.

The whole episode was over in moments.

Charlie stared at Wang and at the fallen pickpockets, his mouth wide-open in disbelief.

"Gotcha!" cried Roy, coming up behind the boy.

As Roy reached for him, Charlie opened wide and chomped down hard on his hand.

"Yeeoww!" cried Roy, jumping back.

Charlie took off, disappearing into the busy market.

Roy chased after him.

Wang scanned the crowd and saw three more pickpockets lurking in the shadows, ready to grab Roy and Charlie. Then he spotted something else: a bicycle! It leaned against a lamppost, one massive wheel in front and a tiny one behind. Wang vaulted up onto the high seat and started pedalling like mad.

He caught up with Charlie just as the boy was pulling away from Roy, a wide, victorious grin on his face. Suddenly, the three pickpockets leapt out of the shadows to surround the boy. Charlie stopped, frozen in place with nowhere to run.

Wang pulled up on the bike, popping a wheelie and whipping the handlebars around. They spun so fast they were nothing but a blur, like a toy top. They mowed all three pickpockets down, strewing them over the cobblestones like sacks of flour.

Wang hopped off the bike.

Charlie tipped his hat. "Cheerio, guv," he said. Then he dropped to the ground and rolled under a cart, heading for freedom once again.

Just then, a tall, lanky ginger-haired man in a tweed suit appeared around the corner, accompanied by six burly policemen.

"Inspector Doyle!" Charlie yelped, skidding to a stop and turning to head the opposite way.

"After him, lads!" cried the inspector.

Desperately, Charlie looked all around, then ducked under a cart piled high with a pyramid of juicy red tomatoes.

Wang could see that the boy needed help. He springboarded up onto the front of the cart, sending its ripe contents shooting up into the air and down again, splattering right onto the seven men. They stood there, dripping with red pulp.

Charlie didn't pause to enjoy the sight. He took off running and made his escape.

The inspector looked around. The market

was in total chaos, with upturned carts spilling their contents and pickpockets and thieves lying all over the cobblestones. He shook his head. Then he looked Roy and Wang up and down, taking in their odd clothes. "I think," he said, "you gentlemen should accompany me back to the Yard."

CHAPTER SEVEN:
Scotland Yard

Wang and Roy sat on opposite sides of a whitewashed chamber, staring at each other through the dusty ray of sun that was its only source of light. The stone floor gave the place a chilly, unforgiving feeling. They'd been in London for less than twenty-four hours, and the two had already ended up in a holding cell at Scotland Yard, headquarters of the Criminal Investigation Department of the London police. How could it have happened?

A key clanked in the massive, barred door. "Let me handle this," Roy said to Wang.

"No," said Wang. "I will handle it."

Roy shook his head. "Look, the English aren't like you. They don't get all emotional and touchy-feely. So park the Kung Fu and let me do the talking."

The door swung open and a policeman walked in, escorting the red-haired inspector. The man in the tweed suit nodded at the two. "Inspector Artie Doyle," he said, introducing himself. "I've been after the Fleet Street Gang for two years. I've gathered a file cabinet of evidence — and you two bring them down in an afternoon. A triumph of brawn over brains. Bravo!"

He flung his arms around a very surprised Roy, then hugged Wang as well. Then he reached into his coat pocket and pulled out Roy's watch. "By the way," he said, "a street urchin turned this in. It's a relief to know that there are still a few honest youngsters out there." He handed it to Roy. "I hope your luck turns around," he added.

Roy frowned. "What do you mean?"

"I deduced from your watch," replied Artie

seriously, "that you've hit a bit of a rough patch."

Wang looked amazed. "He has. How did you know?"

Artie tried to look casual. "It's an investigative technique I've developed. I can deduce intimate details about a person through close scrutiny of their personal effects."

Yanking the watch out of Roy's hands, Wang handed it to Doyle. "What else can you tell?" he asked eagerly.

Artie took a good look at the timepiece, turning it over in his hands and holding it up to the light. Finally, he said, "The owner of this watch is a bad gambler and a lousy shot. Although he has cheated death several times, he spends most of his life wandering from place to place in a futile search for purpose and respect." He paused.

Wang was stunned. "That," he said, "is amazing."

Roy wasn't impressed. "Yeah, amazingly *off!* It doesn't sound anything like me." He grabbed the watch back and tucked it into his pocket.

Artie gave a little cough. "Well," he said,

embarrassed, "I'm still working out the kinks in my technique."

Roy gave him a forgiving smile. "No offense," he said. "I'm sure that's a real popular party trick. But for the record, I'm Roy O' Bannon."

Artie took a step back. "You're Roy O' Bannon, the famous Western folk hero? I've read *Roy O' Bannon Versus the Mummy* five times!"

"This here's the Shanghai Kid," Roy said, pointing at Wang.

"Ah, yes," said Artie. "The faithful Chinese sidekick."

You could practically see the steam coming out of Wang's ears. "I am not a sidekick! Those stories are all lies!"

"He's a little sensitive," Roy apologized for his friend. "Don't be bitter," he told Wang. "I didn't write those books. Blame that loon Sage McAllister."

"Well," Artie said, "since you're here, Mr. O' Bannon, perhaps you can help us with a case. Most perplexing. A murderous fiend who calls himself Jack the Ripper . . ."

"Look," Roy interrupted. "No offense, but I'm kind of dealing with my own problems now, figuring out my future and all. And we're looking for John's sister."

"I must find her," Wang added urgently. He pulled the letter out of his pocket. "She's staying at this address. Can you take us there?"

Artie looked at the envelope, and his face fell. "Oh, dear," he muttered. Then he looked at Wang. "I think you'd better come with me." He led the two men out of their cell and down a dank, dreary hall. He pulled a key out of his pocket, opened another cell door, and pushed the creaking door open. Wang and Roy stepped into the dimly lit cell and walked over to the shadowy figure lying on the mattress beneath the window, only to find that it was just a jacket, stuffed with straw.

In the next instant, a figure somersaulted down from the ceiling, launching a scissor-kick at the three men and sending them tumbling to the floor. A sweeper-kick came next, aimed straight at Roy's head.

CHAPTER EIGHT:
Chon Lin

Wang snaked out a quick hand to catch the deadly foot, just before it connected.

"Chon Lin!" he said.

"Chon Wang?" asked the girl, turning to see her brother. She ran into his arms, and they embraced for a long moment as Roy and Artie picked themselves up off the floor.

"Well," Artie said, clearing his throat. "I'll leave you all alone." He stepped out of the cell, unnoticed.

Roy was staring at Chon Lin. There was no mistaking the look in his eyes. It was love at first sight. "So, John," he said, rubbing his head. "Are you going to introduce me to your sister?"

Wang glanced at Roy. "This is Chon Lin," he said. "My baby sister."

"I am not a baby!" Chon Lin snapped.

Roy looked her up and down. "I'll tell you one thing, John, she certainly doesn't take after you in the looks department." He smiled at Chon Lin. She smiled back.

In Chinese, Chon Lin asked her brother, *"Is this the American sidekick you wrote about in your letters? You never mentioned that he was so charming."*

Roy wagged a finger. "Now, now," he said, "no talking about me in your native tongue."

Wang rolled his eyes and stepped between his friend and his sister. "Why are you in this cell?" he asked Chon Lin.

She gave him a level look. "I followed the man who murdered Father," she began. Then she stopped.

"Well?" Wang asked.

Hesitatingly, she finished. "And when I found out where he lived, I snuck inside his house and tried to kill him!"

Roy shook his head. "I see that hot-tempered thing runs in the Wayne family."

Wang was looking angry. "It is *my* duty to avenge Father's death!" he said to his sister.

"No," she insisted. "It is mine. I am the one who promised him."

"But I am his only son!" said Wang. His eyes radiated intensity.

Chon Lin didn't let up. "When you abandoned us for America, Father said he *had* no son!"

"Whoa," Roy said, holding up his hands in a T. "Time out."

The siblings ignored him. Wang glared at Lin, and she glared back at her brother.

Finally, Roy stepped between them, facing Wang. "Look, John," he said, in a low voice. "Let me work on that detective. He thinks I'm a big celebrity. I bet I can talk us all out of here."

Wang gave his sister one more glare, then went over to bang on the door.

Roy stepped over to Chon Lin. Speaking

gently as he handed her a deck of cards, he said, "Here. Don't be afraid. Occupy yourself."

Chon Lin accepted the cards, but her eyes were still on Wang. "Have you opened Father's box?" she asked.

Over at the door, Wang didn't even turn to answer. "Not yet," he said, just as a guard opened the door. He and Roy stepped out. Behind them, unnoticed, Chon Lin slipped one of the playing cards into the lock as the door closed.

Roy and Wang were escorted to Inspector Doyle's office, where they found Artie reading the paper. "Lord Survives Assassin's Blade!" screamed a bold, black headline. He explained more about Chon Lin's crime. "She tried to assassinate Lord Rathbone while he was having his afternoon tea," he said, pointing to the elegant blond man pictured on the front page.

"Wow," Roy said. "That's a great jacket."

Artie ignored this. "He's tenth in line to the throne and Her Majesty's favorite cousin. The newspapers had a field day."

"What about my sister?" Wang asked, still focused on helping Lin.

Artie paused to light a big, hook-stemmed pipe. Puffing away, he said, "I'm afraid there isn't much you can do for her. She made some preposterous claim that Lord Rathbone murdered your father in China."

Wang didn't blink. "If she said he did, then he did."

Artie put down the pipe and turned his attention to a plateful of cookies. Helping himself to one, he said, "Take my advice, don't go around accusing members of the royal family of murder."

Roy spoke up. "Look, Artie, Lin's not a killer," he pleaded. "She's just a really, really confused girl." He ignored the look Wang gave him. "How about if we get her out of here?"

"I'm afraid that's out of the question," Artie told him stiffly.

Wang frowned. "What will happen to my sister?"

"She'll go to trial," Artie answered, "and probably end up locked away in an institute for the criminally insane. The tabloids have already dubbed her 'Loony Lin.' I thought that was rather catchy." He caught the look

Wang gave him. "At the time, I mean," he added hastily. "Biscuit, anyone?"

That did it. A few moments later, Wang burst out of the main entrance of Scotland Yard. Roy ran after him. "John, wait up!" Roy cried. Wang didn't even turn around. "Where are you going?"

"To find Rathbone," Wang said.

"So you can end up in jail, too?" Roy hurried along next to his friend.

"He killed my father."

Roy exploded. "And if you kill that guy, you'll be the most hated man in England! These people aren't civilized, John. Back home, they'd just hang you. Here, they'll put you on a rack and rip you apart."

Wang's expression didn't change. "I cannot let my sister stay in prison," he said.

Roy's face softened. "I know just how you feel. You want to take her in your arms, hold her close and whisper in her ear that everything's going to be okay," he murmured gently. Then he saw Wang staring at him. "Oops. Did I say that out loud?"

"Stay away from Lin," Wang warned him. Pulling out his puzzle box, he continued to walk down the street at a fast clip. Roy followed him. They turned a corner to find themselves staring up at a huge palace.

"Look at that!" Roy said, his eyes wide. "Buckingham Palace. That's where the queen lives." Wang was still toying with the puzzle box. "C'mon, John," Roy said, "put the box away. You're not going to figure it out when you're angry." He pulled his friend along, walking right up to a guard standing at attention outside the palace. The man stood ramrod straight, his tall black fur-covered helmet nearly covering his eyes. He didn't move a muscle as the two men approached.

"Get a load of this guy," Roy said, taking in the red uniform, the spit-shined boots, the brass buttons.

"Roy, he is a royal guard," Wang said.

Roy nodded. "I read about these guys," he said. "They have to stand outside the palace come rain or shine. You can make faces, insult them — anything! They can't move a muscle."

Remembering his time as an Imperial Guard, Wang answered, "He has a very important job. I used to be one, remember?"

"These guys aren't like you, John," Roy told him. "They're a tourist attraction. Watch." He stepped right in front of the guard. The man ignored him. "Hey, buddy," Roy said. "Your shoe's untied."

The man kept staring straight ahead.

"What's with the goofy hat?" Roy asked. He started waving his hands in front of the guard's face. The man didn't flinch. Roy kept waving as Wang tried to pull him away. "Going to take that from a colonial?" he asked the man. "Come on, take a swing." Roy got right up into the man's face. "Look," he said, pointing to the right. "The queen!"

The man didn't blink.

"Wow," Roy said. "Bet you're an amazing poker player. Oh, well, no hard feelings." He patted the guard on the shoulder.

At that, the guard swung his rifle up, smashing into Roy's stomach.

"*Oof!*" said Roy, as the guard swung the rifle back down, snapping it into place. Once again, he looked like a statue, standing as straight as ever with his face a perfect blank.

"He's not allowed to do that!" Roy gasped.

"You shouldn't have touched him, guv!"

Roy turned to see Charlie grinning up at him. The boy tipped his bowler.

"Scram, punk," Roy said. "We've got friends at Scotland Yard. I'll give you up in a heartbeat."

"You mean Doyle?" asked Charlie. "The man couldn't find his own face in a looking glass." He smiled at Roy. "You get your watch back?"

"You should not steal," Wang told the boy.

Charlie shrugged. "If I don't steal, I don't eat. By the way, who showed you how to do all that kicking and punching?" He started imitating Wang's moves.

"My father," Wang answered.

Charlie noticed the tone in Wang's voice. He quit kicking.

"Hit the road, kid," Roy told him. "We've got important grown-up things to do." Just then, it began to rain — hard. Roy glared up at the sky, hating England with all his heart.

"You need a place to stay?" Charlie asked.

CHAPTER NINE:
Living Large

"Come on in," Charlie said, opening the door of a fancy townhouse. He was covered in soot from entering through the chimney.

Shivering and soaked, Roy and Wang squished across the marble floor, looking around. The place was like nothing they'd ever seen. From the huge, open hall they could see dark wood staircases and doors leading to rooms full of furniture, all covered with white sheets. "Let me guess," Roy said to Charlie. "You're really a prince dressed as a pauper and this is your folks' house."

"My parents are dead," Charlie told him. "The house belongs to a major general who got called back to India. I was sleeping on the street outside when he headed out last week." He beckoned them along, leading them into the parlor.

It didn't take long for Roy to make himself comfortable. After a warm bath, he dressed in the major's smoking gown and plopped himself down in the major's easy chair in front of the major's fire, eating the major's food. He was reaching out to take the last of the major's chocolates when Charlie spoke up.

"Hey, that was mine!" Charlie said.

Roy just raised an eyebrow. "Kid, you've got to learn to look out for number one." With that, he popped the chocolate into his mouth, sighing with contentment. He looked around. "I could settle down in a house like this," he said. "Live the life of a gentleman. Paint pictures while Lin plays with the kids in the garden."

"Who's Lin?" Charlie asked.

Roy smiled. "My future wife," he answered,

just before Wang came into the room, dressed in a robe and slippers. "Check out my new threads, John," Roy said to him. "All that's missing is a loyal hound curled up at my feet."

Wang warmed his hands at the fire. "We are wasting time," he said. "We must find Rathbone."

"What do you think I've been doing down here?" Roy asked. "I've been working on a plan." He snapped his fingers, and Charlie handed him a scroll. He unrolled it. "I figured if we found the Seal, we could prove Rathbone killed your dad." He showed the scroll to Wang. It featured a sketch of a castle, with a scrawled caption reading "Rathbone's Place." On the right was a picture of a catapult, tossing two stick figures named "Roy" and "John" toward the castle. "Now," Roy explained, "we're going to need to calculate the wind speed perfectly, but other than that —"

Before he could finish, Wang grabbed the scroll out of his hands and threw it into the fire.

"Hey!" Roy objected. "I spent at least twenty minutes on that plan."

"It will never work."

"Okay, John," Roy said. "I'm all ears. Dazzle me with some of your mysterious Chinese wisdom." He leaned back in his chair.

Wang ignored the sarcasm. "We should go to his house and look around until we find the Seal."

Roy rolled his eyes. "Okay, not to poke holes, but that's kind of the core idea of my plan."

Meanwhile, Charlie was looking at the society invitations propped on the mantelpiece over the fire. "You don't need a catapult," he said.

"You've seen the security around these castles," Roy said. "How do you plan on getting in?"

Charlie reached out to pluck one of the invitations off the mantle. He read out loud. "Lord Nelson Rathbone requests the pleasure of your company at the Jubilee Ball in honor of Her Majesty's fiftieth year on the throne . . ."

Wang smiled at Charlie as he took the invitation. "Good thinking," he said. He picked up Charlie's hat, spun it around on his finger, and set it back on Charlie's head.

Roy wasn't impressed. "I see some of my influence is rubbing off on you," he said. "Now, all we need is a proper disguise. How about if I go dressed like the major general, and John, you go as my valet?"

Wang didn't skip a beat. "How about if *I* am the major general and *you* are the valet?"

"John," Roy said, exasperated. "You've really got to get over this sidekick thing. Let's face it, you're not exactly English-looking."

"I will not go as a valet," Wang insisted, folding his arms stubbornly.

Roy glanced up at the colorful painting hanging over the mantle, a portrait of a handsome Indian prince. His expression grew thoughtful.

CHAPTER TEN:
The House of Rathbone

"Incredible!" Roy said to Wang as their horse-drawn carriage clattered over the cobblestones and up the long, straight drive to Rathbone's castle. Flaming torches lit their way, and above them the massive building loomed in the darkening sky, a huge heap of stone piled into turrets and ramparts and battlements of every shape and description. They drew closer and closer, until finally their carriage thundered over the drawbridge and beneath the immense, fortified gate known as a barbican.

Welcoming lights and the sound of music and laughter drifted out of the grand hall as the carriage pulled in front of the main entrance. As soon as the horses stopped, Charlie, dressed in a fancy footman's uniform, jumped down from his perch with the driver and opened the carriage doors.

Wang and Roy stepped out.

"I feel like a fool," Wang said, looking down at his flowing silk robe. His peacock-blue turban bobbed as he glanced over at Roy, who was wearing the major's full dress uniform: pointy, feather-plumed hat, brass buttons, and all.

"You're a maharaja," Roy pointed out. "That's Indian royalty."

"But I am Chinese," Wang reminded him.

Roy sighed. "John, you've got to open your mind to other cultures. Now, let's try out our English accents. Listen and learn." He cleared his throat. "How do you do, your lordship," he said, sounding exactly as he always did.

Wang raised an eyebrow. "You sound like you always do," he said.

Roy looked impatient. "John, you're obviously not listening to the cadence of my voice. It's real subtle." He tried again. "How do you do, your lordship?"

Wang shook his head.

"Well, you try it!" John told him.

Wang took a breath. "How do you do, your lordship?" he said, in a perfect English accent.

Roy's jaw fell open. "Okay, new plan," he said hastily. "Let's skip the accents. Now, what are you going to do if you see Rathbone?"

"Kill him." Wang's eyes flashed.

Roy stopped in his tracks, shaking his head. "You're going to have to be civil, because we don't have the Seal yet. No Seal, no Lin, no family honor. Right?" he reminded his friend. As he looked over at Wang, he noticed that Charlie was following them. "Amscray, kid," he told the boy.

"I want to go inside," Charlie insisted. "They say the place is haunted."

But Roy sent him back to the carriage, telling him they needed him to be ready to drive if they had to make a quick getaway. Then he and Wang headed for the ivy-covered entrance.

Inside, all was light and warmth and cheer. Throngs of gaily dressed people stood around talking in perfect British accents at the top of their lungs. The place was packed with ornate furniture, fireplaces big enough to roast an ox in, and gigantic portraits, like the life-sized one of Rathbone that hung right over the master-at-arms, who stood waiting to announce them.

"Tacky," said Roy, looking up at the painting.

"Your name, please?" asked the master-at-arms.

Roy stammered for a moment, having forgotten to come up with a name for himself. He looked around wildly. Then he spotted some words stenciled on the face of an elegant grandfather clock that stood in the hall. "Sherlock Watchmakers," it said. "Holmes County, Ireland."

"Uh, Sherlock Holmes," Roy said quickly.

The master-at-arms turned to Wang. "And what province do you represent, Your Highness?"

Wang didn't skip a beat. "Nevada."

The master-at-arms escorted them to the Great Hall. As they entered, he announced in a deep voice, "May I present Sergeant Major Sherlock Holmes and His Highness the Maharaja of Nevada."

Only a few faces turned to look at them. A crowd of richly dressed people milled around the banquet tables, which were covered with sumptuous delicacies and decorated with ribbons and wreaths of gold. Across the room, Artie Doyle was one of those few faces. He stared at the two as if trying to remember where he'd seen them before.

Roy and Wang stood near the banquet table, looking down at a whole roast pig on a silver platter. A rosy apple filled its mouth. "Okay," said Roy. "Here's the plan. We get some chow, sneak out of the party, and start looking for the Seal." He grabbed a plate. "Mmm, sausage," he said, spearing a few links onto his plate and taking a big bite of one of them. "Not bad. I thought English food was supposed to be awful."

The server smiled. "The haggis is fresh

from Scotland, sir," he said. "It's made with the finest sheep's bladders."

"Phhht!" Roy spit the haggis out onto his plate and handed it back to the server. Then he went to see what Wang was eating. "John, stop!" he said, when he saw Wang chewing on a pig's foot. "You don't know what you're eating!"

Wang smiled contentedly. "I have not had food this good since I left China," he said, chewing happily.

Roy looked disgusted. He stalked off. Wang shrugged and turned back to the pig. He was about to cut off its ear when Rathbone appeared next to him.

"You should try the quail," suggested the lord. "I shot them myself this morning."

Wang turned slowly, staring into Rathbone's face. His hand tightened on the serving knife he held, tightened until the knuckles turned white. Somehow, he managed to keep himself from leaping at Rathbone's neck. "How do you do, your lordship?" he said, in his perfect accent.

"Very well, thank you," said Rathbone. "I

am not acquainted with the Nevada province, but I haven't been to India since eighty-one. I spend most of my time in the Orient."

Wang's eyes were dark with fury, his face a blank. "I hear you just returned from China," he said evenly.

"You are well-informed, Maharaja," Lord Rathbone said. "It is my dream that the Chinese will follow India's example and one day embrace British rule."

Wang didn't blink. "The Chinese are a very proud people," he said slowly. "They place honor and family above all else."

Rathbone's smile was chilling. "I'm sure we'll break them of that," he answered. Then he glanced at the clock. It was eleven-thirty. "If you'll excuse me," he said to Wang, "I have a matter to attend to."

Through gritted teeth, Wang answered, "Until we meet again."

Rathbone walked away, and Roy came over to join his friend. "I'm proud of you, John," he said. He knew what kind of self-control it had taken for Wang to have that simple conversation.

Wang didn't turn to look at Roy. His eyes were burning into Rathbone's back. "We must find the Seal," he said.

Roy nodded. "First, we've got to find somewhere to hide until this crowd thins out."

CHAPTER ELEVEN:
A Long Knight

It was almost midnight when Rathbone strode down a dark hall lit only by the eerie glow of flickering gaslights. Two royal guards marched along with him until he dismissed them with a curt, "That will be all."

Rathbone disappeared through a massive wooden door. The guards turned back, heading past a display of medieval arms and armor as they made for the main palace.

"Ahhh-choo!" A sneeze echoed through the dark hall.

The guards stopped in their tracks.

"Ahhh-choo!" Another sneeze.

One of the guards bent towards a suit of armor for a closer look.

Crash! The armor came to life, lunged for the guard, missed him completely, and fell thrashing to the floor.

As the guards watched in complete disbelief, another suit of armor came to life behind them, jumping off its pedestal with a loud rattle. When the guards turned to look, the reanimated knight launched into a pivot-kick, smashing one of them to the ground.

For a moment, the other guard could only stare. The rusty old armor had left the knight's leg sticking straight out, frozen in the moment of the kick. Then the guard snatched a staff from a row displayed on the wall and speared the knight's helmet, ripping it right off the rest of the suit of armor.

In place of the helmet was . . . air.

Nothingness.

The guard began to shake with fear as he stared at the headless knight. Then the knight came to life again, hopping onto its other foot and sweeping a swift kick at the guard, knocking him out.

Wang's head popped out of the suit. Surveying the scene quickly, he stepped over to the fallen knight and lifted the visor.

Roy blinked. "How many did I get?" he asked.

Wang took pity on him and lied. "You got one and I got one."

Grinning groggily, Roy fell for it. "See, even in a tin can," he said, "I've got the moves of a lithe cat."

They shucked their armor and headed down the hall to the spot where they'd last seen Rathbone. Peering into Rathbone's private library through the keyhole of the massive doors, Roy reported, "He just pulled a fancy dragon key out of his desk!"

Wang grimaced. "That was my father's! I must avenge his honor!" He reached for the door handle.

Roy tried to stop him, grabbing his hand. "C'mon, John, quit going all Chinese on me!"

But he was too late. Wang threw himself against the door, bursting it open and exploding into the room.

The library was empty.

Frozen in his tracks, Wang peered around the quiet, book-lined room. "Where did he go?"

Roy joined him. "There aren't any windows, and we just came through the door. That leaves only one explanation. In *Roy O' Bannon Versus the Mummy,* remember how the zombie king got away when I chased him into the pharoah's tomb?"

Wang rolled his eyes. "How could I?" he asked. "I was busy watering the camels."

Roy blushed. "Oh, yeah. Well, there was a secret passageway hidden behind the sphinx." He looked around the room. "There must be a secret lever or button hidden around here somewhere."

Wang couldn't believe his ears. "That is the stupidest thing I have ever heard," he said.

"You got a better idea?" Roy asked. "C'mon, start picking stuff up." He grabbed a leather-bound volume off the nearest shelf. Nothing happened. Then he started grabbing other things — a paperweight, a dictionary on a stand, a gas lamp — as fast as he could. Meanwhile, Wang began to search Rathbone's desk.

Suddenly, Wang grew still. He looked up at a painting hanging on the wall, a portrait of a little child playing on a lawn. The eyes of the child were staring right at him — and they weren't painted! They were most definitely human.

"Roy," he hissed. "The painting. It is looking at me."

Roy glanced up at the painting. Suddenly, it looked normal again, with the eyes painted in. "John, you're starting to sound like Charlie. The house isn't haunted. Keep searching."

Wang went over to check out a row of statues along one wall while Roy pulled a book off the shelf and started leafing through it, looking at the pictures. Wang glanced up at a portrait of a hunting dog. The dog's eyes were staring right back at him!

"Roy!" Wang whispered urgently.

Roy didn't look up from his book. "What is it now, John? Are the statues moving?"

Wang was speechless, staring at those eyes. He backed into a statue of a naked woman. Suddenly, the nearby fireplace revolved around on a turntable, shooting Wang out of the library and into a large stone chamber lit by the flickering glow of flaming torches.

The light glinted off the treasures in the room, treasures that Rathbone had plundered from every corner of the world. Wang stared at the chests full of jewels, the ancient artifacts, the brocaded tapestries. Then he saw what he was looking for.

The dragon key.

It was in the keyhole of a very familiar golden box.

The box that held the Seal.

Wang stepped towards it. Then, out of the corner of his eye, he caught the glint of metal, reflected on a priceless Aztec shield.

Wang spun away.

A sword swept down, just missing him.

Wang glanced around and took in the three royal guards advancing towards him, each man armed with a long, shining sword. They came at him, swinging.

Wang grabbed the shield and blocked their strokes. *Clang! Clang!* The guards backed him into a corner. Aiming the shield like a Frisbee, Wang threw it at one of the guards, slicing him down and sending him reeling into an Egyptian sarcophagus. The lid slammed shut, trapping the guard inside.

Moving quickly, Wang grabbed two medieval spiked clubs from their display brackets and spun them like lightning, fending off the two other guards as he made his way back toward the fireplace.

The turntable spun back into the library, carrying Wang — and the guards, who had jumped aboard! "Roy!" Wang shouted.

Roy was still engrossed in his book. "For the last time," he said, without looking up, "the pictures aren't looking at you."

Wang didn't even get a chance to speak before one of the guards bumped the statue, sending the turntable spinning again.

Roy was left alone in the silent room. Finally, he looked up and saw that his friend had disappeared. "John?" he called. He peered into the eyes of a portrait of an old Elizabethan woman. "John, is that you?"

Just then, the two guards they'd left in the hall burst into the room. Roy grabbed a spear from the wall. "Back for more? Okay, bring it on!"

The guards attacked. Roy held up the spear to fend off their blows, but their swords chopped right through it. *Wham! Wham! Wham!* In three strokes, the spear was nothing but matchsticks. The guards backed Roy up, right against the portrait he'd been looking at. "All right, John!" Roy shouted to the painting. "Fun and games are over! I could use a little help right about now."

The guards raised their swords. They were on the brink of slicing Roy in half when suddenly the portrait tore open.

Chon Lin exploded out into the room, feet and hands flying. She backflipped towards the guards and swept a lightning-fast kick into their faces, sending them crashing to the floor.

"That's amazing!" Roy cried, love lighting up his eyes as he stared at Lin. "I was just thinking about you. You're my sugar magnolia. You could fight all my battles for me."

Meanwhile, inside the secret chamber of treasures, Wang was still fighting for his life. Once again, the guards had backed him into the fireplace. He fumbled for the lever that would spin him back to the library and Roy, but it was just out of reach.

The guards drew closer, their swords flashing in the gaslight as they lifted them high for the final blow.

CHAPTER TWELVE:
The Missing Seal

In the library, Chon Lin strode towards the fireplace and pushed against the statue. The turntable spun, throwing her and Roy into the chamber while Wang and the guards were pitched back into the library.

Wang moved quickly as the guards fought to get their balance back, diving to the floor and rolling as far as he could.

It wasn't far enough.

The guards came after him.

Wang scrambled up a ladder that was leaning against the bookshelves.

With a roar, the guards came after him.

Wang flipped the ladder along the row of shelves, moving with incredible skill until he came to the end of the room. The guards caught up to him, swinging their swords wildly and cutting the ladder in half.

Wang crashed back down to the floor.

The guards came closer.

Grabbing half the ladder with his feet, Wang spun it into his hands and wrenched it down over their swords. When their arms were locked into the rungs, Wang whipped the ladder around, sending their swords flying. Then Wang pulled the ladder back and with a huge heave, thrust it at one of the guards, throwing him into a bookshelf. A thunderous avalanche of books tumbled down, burying the man. Wang didn't pause. He thrust the ladder again, launching the other guard high into the air and right through a painting.

Without glancing back, Wang headed for the fireplace. Pushing on the statue, he spun himself around, only to come face-to-face with Roy and Chon Lin.

"Hey, where have you been?" Roy asked. "Look who I found."

"Chon Lin," Wang said, looking at his sister.

Roy could hardly contain himself. "John, you should see her fight. I mean, you're pretty good, but when I saw *her* in action —"

Wang wasn't listening. In two long steps, he moved to the gold chest. Turning the dragon key, he opened the lid — and his face fell.

"The Seal is gone," he said.

Quickly, he looked around the room. How could the Seal have disappeared so fast? His eye was caught by a flickering torch. He leapt to his feet and strode over to it, ripping away the medieval tapestry that hung nearby.

Behind the tapestry was a stone stairway.

"Follow me!" Wang said, grabbing a torch and heading into the passage.

Meanwhile, Rathbone walked down the aisle of his private stables. It was midnight.

As noiselessly as a cat, Wu Yip appeared out of the shadows.

"Must you keep doing that?" Rathbone asked, startled.

Wu Yip did not smile. "I was taught not to be seen or heard. Did you bring the Seal?"

"I am a man of my word," said Rathbone, as he pulled the Seal from his coat and handed it to the thin Chinese man.

Wu Yip took the Seal, handling it reverently. Looking down at it, he said softly, "I remember watching my brother play with this like a baby's rattle." Then his voice changed. "When I tried to touch it, the dowager empress beat me."

Rathbone gave him a wicked smile. "No doubt your deprived childhood made you the man you are today."

Wu Yip looked up at him and smiled back.

In the next stall over, a chestnut mare nibbled her oats. She snorted suddenly and reared her head back as her stone trough slid away, revealing a stone staircase. As the mare watched curiously, three figures climbed out. They tiptoed to the corner of the stall and peered around it.

"Wu Yip," Wang said, his eyes narrowing when he saw the man with Rathbone.

"Wu who?" Roy asked.

"The emperor's half brother," Wang whispered. "He was banished from the Forbidden City for trying to steal the Seal."

Chon Lin finished the story. "Our father caught him," she told Roy. "Wu Yip vowed he would return and claim the emperor's throne."

The three watched as Wu Yip passed the Seal back to Rathbone. The sparkle of the immense diamond caught Roy's eye. He grabbed Wang's robe. "You didn't mention the gigantic diamond," he hissed.

"Do not get any ideas, Roy," Wang cautioned.

"What?" Roy asked, doing his best to look innocent. "I was just admiring the craftsmanship."

Suddenly, Wang looked around. "Where is Chon Lin?" he whispered.

Just then, a loud neigh broke the quiet of the stable.

"Get out!" Rathbone ordered Wu Yip. The Chinese man disappeared into the shadows.

Rathbone turned back, just in time to see the strong, slim figure of Chon Lin flying at him, feetfirst.

CHAPTER THIRTEEN:
All Fired Up

"You murdered my father!" Chon Lin cried, crashing into Rathbone. The Seal fell out of his hands, skittering into a nearby stall. Rathbone swept a kick at the girl, knocking her to the ground.

Roy dove for the Seal.

Zing! Crash! A bullet whizzed through the air, missing Roy and Chon Lin by a hair as it shattered a lantern, sending flames flying into the straw-strewn floor. Instantly, a roaring fire filled the stall.

Rathbone swung around, scanning the stables as he held his pistol at the ready. He spotted Wang and started to shoot.

Meanwhile, Roy managed to stagger to his feet. Something caught his eye: the glint of a diamond in the firelight. He took a step nearer to the Seal.

Out of the darkness burst a small figure: Charlie! Without missing a step, he grabbed the Seal before Roy could reach it.

"Come back, you little punk!" roared Roy.

"Sorry, guv," Charlie shot back over his shoulder. "I'm looking out for number one." He raced away — but not before Roy reached out and snatched the old black bowler off his head.

Frustrated, Roy punched the hat, just as Wang turned up at his side. "The punk's got the Seal," Roy reported.

Helplessly, he and Wang stared into the flames. Through the flickering curtain, they made out the figure of Chon Lin. In one smooth move, she grabbed the mane of a panicking, galloping horse and flung herself astride it as it burst out of the stables.

A coughing Rathbone staggered out as

well. He watched as several other terrified horses escaped. Then he slammed the door of the stables and swung down the thick wooden arm, locking Wang and Roy inside the raging inferno.

Seconds later, the door slammed open as Rathbone's prized Mercedes Benz automobile exploded out of the stables, Roy at the wheel and Wang hanging on for dear life in the passenger seat. Flaming chunks of wood flew through the air as the car careened through the stableyard. Behind it, the stable roof collapsed, sending a column of sparks high into the night air.

Meanwhile, on the other side of Rathbone's castle, Artie Doyle paced along looking into the moat. All was quiet and serene — until the car hurtled through the gate, forcing him to belly flop into the dark, stagnant water!

"Yeee-hawww!" Roy yodeled, as he spun the wheel.

"Roy, slow down," Wang shouted.

Roy was totally pumped. "John," he yelled, "this machine was built for speed." He glanced at the dashboard and all the dials. "Besides," he admitted, "I'm not sure where the brake thing is."

"Look out!" Wang cried, reaching over to jerk the steering wheel hard to the left. They swerved just in time to miss a carriage that was headed straight for them on the narrow roadway.

Suddenly, the car jounced off the road and dove into the woods. Whipped by branches, it coasted on a crazy slalom course through the trees.

"You are a very bad driver," Wang managed to inform Roy. They both ducked as the car plowed through a wooden fence, smashing its headlights. The car kept rolling through the darkness. Roy sat up to glance around at the moonlit scene.

"Don't worry, John," he said, seeing that they were in the midst of an open meadow. "It's smooth sailing from here." He put the pedal to the metal and the car lurched forward, slamming straight into a solid stone wall.

CHAPTER FOURTEEN: Sweet Dreams

Roy stretched and turned over, enjoying the smooth, cool luxury of the silken sheets that surrounded him. The soft pillow under his head felt wonderful. And it was quiet and peaceful. This was better than a room at Waldorf.

"Baaahhhh!"

Someone was yelling and knocking on the door. The knocking grew louder, louder.

"Baaahhhh!"

"Just a few more minutes." Roy muttered, trying to roll over and go back to sleep.

"Roy, wake up!"

It was Wang's voice.

At that moment, Roy woke up for real. He was sitting in the driver's seat of a totaled Mercedes, his arms wrapped around a smelly, woolly sheep that had climbed in to join him.

"Ahhh!" Roy cried, pushing the sheep away. He sat up to look around and saw that the car had crashed into one of a circle of giant stone slabs that stood in the middle of a meadow. Next to him, Wang stared too, mystified at the sight.

"Who would leave a pile of stones in the middle of a field?" Wang asked.

"I don't know, John," Roy answered wearily. "These people are nuts."

They climbed out of the car and began to walk out of the meadow, past a cluster of grazing sheep. "Roy," Wang said, "when you were asleep, you called out my sister's name."

Roy answered quickly. "You're not going to believe this," he said, "but 'Lynn's' also my mother's name."

"I do not believe you." Wang said suspiciously.

Roy stammered. "John, I was just in an accident. I'm confused. I probably have a concussion." He paused. "But now that we're on the subject, was she seeing anyone in China?"

Wang's eyes flashed. "Stay away from Lin."

"Would it be so bad to have me as family?" Roy pleaded. "We'd see each other at holidays, take our kids to karate class . . ."

Wang looked straight ahead, expressionless. "If you date my sister, I will break your legs."

Roy winced. "You know, you've got to stop the cycle of aggression in your family."

Just then, they found themselves at the top of a grassy mound. In the distance, a horse-drawn carriage rumbled towards them.

"Get your thumb out, Maharaja," Roy said joyfully. "Looks like we're hitching back to town."

The carriage drew closer and came to a stop in front of them. The driver, up on a high seat in front of the carriage, gave them a tip of the hat.

Black hair tumbled loose around the driver's face. It was Chon Lin!

Roy grinned up at her. "You're fast becoming my favorite Wayne."

Chon Lin blushed. A disgusted Wang just shook his head.

Roy and Wang climbed aboard, sitting up front with Chon Lin as she took the reins and the horses began to trot. The carriage trundled along through the brilliant green hills and dales of the English countryside. When Wang pulled out his puzzle box and began to fiddle with it, Roy scooted over to be a bit closer to Chon Lin.

"This your first time in England?" he asked, starting a conversation. When Chon Lin nodded shyly, he went on. "I'm impressed. You really know your way around."

Chon Lin blushed again. "I've always had a good sense of direction," she said.

Roy raised an eyebrow and glanced over at Wang. "Really," he said, "Because your brother can't tell which way is up. One time I sent him over a mountain range."

That made Chon Lin smile. "One time I sent him over the Great Wall," she confided. "He was lost for three days."

Wang tried to ignore their laughter.

"We've got so much in common," Roy told Chon Lin.

She gazed into his eyes. "I've never met anybody like you, Roy," she sighed.

"Really?" Roy asked. "Hey, do you like Chinese food?"

Wang gave an exasperated snort. He put the puzzle box away and, as Roy moved even closer to Chon Lin, Wang vaulted up and over his friend, swinging into the spot between them on the driver's bench. "We must find Charlie and get the Seal," he said, all focus and determination.

Chon Lin glared at him.

Roy muttered under his breath.

And the carriage trundled on.

CHAPTER FIFTEEN:
The Truth Comes Out

As night fell, the carriage bumped over a busy London street, dodging vendors and beggars as it rolled beneath an arch reading "Whitechapel."

"Looks like a nice enough neighborhood for a hideout," Roy said, as Chon Lin pulled the carriage up in front of the Puss 'n' Boots Inn, a tumbledown boardinghouse.

Wang didn't like the look of the place. "I will not let my sister stay here," he said.

Roy pointed out that if they checked in anywhere else, they'd be arrested before they got to their room.

"Anyway, I don't mind this place," said Chon Lin. She led the way into the inn.

Roy followed her like a puppy follows its master. Wang glared at him. "She's so wonderful, John," Roy said to his friend. "I think I found my key."

"Roy," Wang warned. "She is my baby sister."

"And I'm your best friend," Roy answered. "C'mon. I've never asked you for anything before in my life. Will you put in a good word for me?" Now he *looked* like a puppy, begging for scraps.

Finally, Wang nodded. "Sure, Roy," he said. "I will tell her the truth."

Roy's face lit up. "Great! Prepare for operation 'sweep her off her feet.'"

The trio checked in and headed upstairs to their rooms, which were right next to each other. Wang and Chon Lin went into one of them. Roy stepped into his room and closed the door.

Roy crept over to the door that linked his room with Wang and Chon Lin's. He pressed his ear to the wood and listened.

"Chon Lin," Wang was saying, "our father talked about the right man for you. He must be strong, courageous, a good father."

"Like Roy," Chon Lin answered.

Roy melted. "That's right," he whispered to himself. "Come on, now, John. Bring it home for your old buddy."

Wang spoke again. "You do not know him like I do. He has many bad habits."

Roy's face fell.

"Such as?" Chon Lin asked.

"He drinks," said Wang. "Smokes, gambles . . ."

Roy couldn't help nodding. His friend wasn't lying.

Chon Lin defended Roy. "But I see inside him," she told her brother. "He has a good heart."

"Chon Lin," Wang said softly. "He cannot be trusted."

On the other side of the door, Roy winced.

"He is your friend," Chon Lin said. "How can you say these things?"

Wang asks Roy for his share of the emperor's gold so that he can go to London. Roy tries to explain that he doesn't have the gold right this minute, but that it's perfectly safe. Wang isn't so sure.

Wang, Roy, and their new sidekick, Charlie, make themselves at home in a major general's mansion. Luckily for them, the major general is in India so he doesn't mind!

How do you crash a high society party? Step one: Get yourself some cool clothes. Roy and Wang prepare for their society debut.

Step two: You need to know how to walk the walk as well as look the part.

Hiding in the stable,
Lin, Wang, and Roy
learn just how far
Rathbone is prepared to
go to become the next
king of England.

Roy's got a plan — maybe that's why Lin looks so worried!

Even though they're outnumbered, Roy and Wang aren't afraid to kick a little butt — at least Wang isn't, Roy's not so sure.

Wang and Roy don't really enjoy hanging around —
especially when there are criminals to be stopped —
but the Boxers they're up against have other ideas!

Wang answered slowly. "Roy is the type of friend you don't introduce to your other friends," he said. "Or bring home to your family."

Roy hung his head.

"I don't care," Chon Lin said stubbornly.

"I forbid it!" Wang shouted.

"You are not my father!" With that, Chon Lin ran out of the room, slamming the door behind her.

In the next room, Roy sat back on his heels, his eyes full of the pain of betrayal.

CHAPTER SIXTEEN:
The Feathers Fly

Wang picked his way through the crowd. The pub was packed! And the customers were not exactly Boy Scouts. They looked like a seedy bunch, the type who'd just as soon pick your pocket as say hello. He used his elbows to fend off the most aggressive beggars, and finally made his way to Roy, who was slumped on a stool, staring into a glass. "Roy," Wang said. "Where have you been? Are you okay? You need anything?"

"Yeah," Roy snapped. "A whole lot of leave me alone."

A guilty look flashed across Wang's face. He tried to smile.

"Come on, Roy. Cheer up." He made some faces and jumped around, trying to make Roy smile.

"It's not working, John," Roy said. "I'm not going to be seduced by your childlike agility." He swung a badly aimed fist in Wang's direction.

Wang didn't even have to duck. But he looked surprised. "Why are you trying to hit me?" he asked.

Roy didn't answer. Instead, he swung again. "You're not the only one who knows Kung Fu. I'm going to kick your butt."

Wang ignored the threat. "What's bothering you?" he asked.

Roy turned to look his friend straight in the eye. "I heard what you said to your sister about me."

A light dawned in Wang's eyes. He bowed his head, ashamed. "Oh," he said softly.

"Yeah," Roy said. "'Oh.' You smashed the

puzzle box of my heart, John. Now I'll never figure out *my* message." He looked down at the table.

Wang flinched. Then he faced his friend. "I will make it right, Roy," he said. "But now I think you should get some sleep."

A few minutes later, Wang led Roy to the door of his room. "Okay," he said, when he'd opened the door. "You'll see it will be all right."

Roy blinked.

"No, John," he said. "I don't think it will be." He turned to walk back out the door.

Wang reached over, grabbed a pillow, and threw it at Roy's head.

Slowly, Roy turned around, a warning look in his eyes. "Do that again," he said seriously, "and I will hurt you."

Wang smirked and threw another pillow. This one hit Roy in the stomach.

Roy bent over to pick it up. He gave Wang a stern look. "I warned you," he said. Then he grinned. "Pillow fight!" he yelled at the top of his lungs.

In moments, the room was filled with a blizzard of flying feathers.

After a few minutes, Wang sat up and spit out a mouthful of feathers. Roy stood and brushed some feathers from his hair.

"Okay," Roy said. "I guess I understand why you said what you did. But I'm really a changed man."

Wang looked doubtful.

"No really," Roy insisted. "You'll see. I really think Chon Lin could be the one. She's everything I . . . hey, where is she?"

Wang looked blank for a moment then leapt to his feet. He and Roy both raced for the door.

CHAPTER SEVENTEEN: Captured

Wang and Roy burst out of the inn, Roy still picking feathers out of his hair. They paused at an intersection, guessing wildly at which direction Chon Lin might have gone. The streets were a maze of narrow, dark alleyways, over which a thick fog was settling. "Lin?" Roy called, his voice fading in the clammy air.

Its echo just reached Lin who was nearby. After running out of the inn, she'd gotten lost in the in the dark mist that surrounded her. Now suddenly, she was feeling very alone and very vulnerable. "Roy?" she said, turning to look for him.

Wang and Roy materialized out of the gloom. "What are you doing?" Roy asked her. "Don't you know it's dangerous out here?"

Relieved to see them both but still angry at her brother, Lin shrugged and turned to stalk off. Suddenly, three silent men loomed in front of her, dressed in black suits and red turbans. She turned around. So did Wang and Roy. Three more men appeared, blocking the end of the bridge the friends had just crossed.

Roy stared at the intimidating figures. "Who *are* these guys?" he asked.

"Boxers." Wang spat the word out contemptuously.

Roy didn't look any less confused. "What did we do to them?"

As if in answer, Lord Rathbone strode out of the fog, looking like his own ghost. "They're with me," he said. He flicked his wrist, and a derringer popped into his hand. Swiftly, he reached out to grab Chon Lin's arms. In one quick move, he spun her around and pressed the weapon against her temple.

Wang and Roy leapt forward.

The Boxers surrounded them.

Rathbone gestured politely. "If you gentlemen would be so kind as to follow me," he said. It was clear that he had somehow learned their true identities, including the fact that Chon Lin was Wang's sister. Holding her hostage was the simplest way to capture all three.

Keeping the gun on Chon Lin, he led them through a labyrinth of streets, towards the river Thames. At last they found themselves in a cavernous warehouse. The river lapped at the other side of a pair of large wooden doors. A barge was docked at the massive indoor loading bay where boxes and crates were stacked high.

A gangplank led from the barge to the dock. As the Boxers forced Roy and Wang to kneel in front of the barge, a figure descended the gangplank.

It was Wu Yip, slender and tall, and as threatening as a coiled cobra.

"Chon Wang," he said with a thin smile. "The man who defied an emperor."

Wang glared at him.

Rathbone motioned to the Boxers. One of them hooked Chon Lin's arms to a roped pulley. Rathbone watched approvingly as the man anchored her legs to the floor, chaining them in place. Then Rathbone turned to Wang and Roy. "Tell me what I want to know or I start pulling her apart," he said. "I know the urchin has the Seal. Where is he?"

Wang spoke up. "We do not know."

Rathbone's lips twitched into something resembling a smile. He signalled to the Boxer and the man yanked down on the rope. It pulled taut, and instantly Chon Lin was stretched out, her face creasing in pain.

Roy yelped. "Enough with the sick torture routine! He's not lying. The little punk kid double-crossed us! He's probably out buying candy for all his chimney sweep pals."

Rathbone gave him a pitying look. "Outwitted by a child," he said. "If you're the best the notorious Wild West has to offer, I think the British Empire is better off without your pathetic country." He signalled again to the Boxer, who yanked on the rope.

Wang lurched forward as if to save his sister, but Wu Yip stomped down hard on his chain, sending him crashing back to the warehouse floor.

Roy faced Wu Yip. "Why do you want this Seal, anyway?" he asked.

Wu Yip answered calmly. "The Seal represents imperial power. I will use it to unite the emperor's enemies and storm the Forbidden City."

On the floor, Wang sat up and stared at Wu Yip. "You will fail," he said flatly.

Roy turned to Rathbone. "What's in it for you?" he asked.

Rathbone smirked. "How about the British Empire?" he asked. He puffed out his chest. "You're looking at the future king of England."

"Ha," Roy scoffed. "Aren't you, like, twentieth in line for the throne?"

"Tenth," Rathbone corrected him. He nodded toward Wu Yip. "But my friend is about to change all that by a simple process of elimination."

Roy cocked his head. "Let me get this straight," he said. "You steal the Seal for him and he's got to pick off nine royals for you?" He turned to Wu Yip. "You really got the bad end of *that* deal!"

Rathbone just smiled. Then he gestured to another Boxer, who whipped a tarp off a lumpy object to reveal a huge, gleaming gun, mounted on a tripod.

Wang and Roy stared at the horrific weapon.

"It's called a machine gun," a proud Rathbone told them, "and it is the first of its kind. It fires five hundred rounds a minute. It's a testament to British ingenuity."

"Were you *born* twisted?" asked Roy.

Once again, Rathbone merely smiled. Then he turned to the Boxers. "Dump them in the river," he barked. He motioned to the Boxers guarding Chon Lin. They unhooked her and headed for the stairs with her body draped over their shoulders.

"Where are you taking her?" Wang roared after them.

Rathbone turned to answer. "To make history," he said. "I can already see the headline: 'Nation Mourns as Loony Lin Massacres Royal Family.'" He and Wu Yip cackled with glee as they headed up the stairs.

Wu Yip couldn't help turning back to put in the last word. "You came all this way to honor your father's name," he said to Wang. "Now, it will be synonymous with cowardice and murder." He smiled a slow, reptilian smile. "Imagine his shame." Then he followed Rathbone up the stairs, and watched as the Boxers shoved Chon Lin into a waiting carriage.

Wang and Roy overheard as he spoke to his partner in crime. "I need your assurance that you will find the Seal," Wu Yip told Rathbone.

"Don't concern yourself," Rathbone answered. "My men are scouring the city."

Wu Yip spoke quietly and firmly. "You better pray they find it by tomorrow night. If not, our agreement is over and you will never get the crown."

CHAPTER EIGHTEEN:
Hanging Around

"John," Roy said, "I've got a confession to make."

Wrists bound, the two friends were hanging upside down over the dark, cold water of the Thames. Their manacled feet were chained to a pair of massive jib-hooks at the end of a long crane arm. A couple of Boxers cranked the arm until it held Roy and Wang high over the water.

Wang twisted to look at his friend. "You are in love with my sister," he guessed.

"Yes," Roy admitted. "But I've got another

confession." He looked at Wang. "It's about the gold," he went on. "I didn't exactly invest it in zeppelins."

"What did you do with it?" Wang asked.

Roy glanced down at the water, then back at his friend. "You know the Roy O' Bannon novels? I wrote them. I'm Sage McAllister."

"You!" Wang was surprised. "But he is old."

"If you take a closer look at the picture on the back of the books, you'll see," Roy told his friend. "It's me in disguise."

"You wrote those lies?" Wang asked.

Roy shrugged, as well as he could while hanging upside down. "I always had a knack for making stuff up," he said. "So I figured I'd be a novelist. But no publisher would take them. So I self-published."

"How many books did you print?" Wang couldn't help being curious.

Roy thought. "About a million," he guessed.

Wang just shook his head.

"I'm sorry, John," Roy said. "I inflated my character in the books so I'd feel better about myself. I've got to be about the worst friend a guy could have."

Wang looked at him. "No," he said. "You are a good friend. I am sorry I said those things about you to Lin. If you really love her, I will not stand in your way." He paused. "But if you break her heart, I will break your legs."

Roy smiled. "You know," he told his friend, "if I wasn't hanging up here, I'd give you a hug."

That brought Wang back to the real world. He looked up at the hooks that held them, then down at the river, then back at the barge. Then he began to swing back and forth on the hook.

"John," Roy said. "You got a plan?"

"Yes," answered Wang, still swinging.

"Anything I need to know?"

"No."

"Okay," Roy said trustingly. "I'll just hang back."

Wang swung higher and higher. Then, when he had enough momentum, he jerked his chain off the hook and somersaulted high over the water, landing with a catlike thump on the deck of the barge.

The Boxers turned and drew their swords.

CHAPTER NINETEEN:
Battle on the Barge

One of the Boxers lunged towards Wang, his sword glinting as he swung the curved blade.

Wang grabbed the chain still attached to his feet and whipped it up and around the blade, stopping it just inches from his face. With a grunt, he wrenched the sword out of the Boxer's hands, sending it flying over the side of the barge. The sword disappeared into the black Thames.

Spinning, Wang bicycle-kicked his manacled feet into the Boxer's back and sent him flying after his sword. The man landed in the water with a huge splash.

"John!" Roy called urgently.

Wang turned, just in time to see another Boxer holding his sword high, ready to slice him in two. Instantly, Wang dropped to his back and raised his legs so that the sword sliced right through his leg chains, stopping at his wrist manacles. Then he swept a foot into the Boxer's face, knocking him backwards. The Boxer fought back, and he and Wang traded blows.

"Hey, John!" Roy called again. "I'm about to buy it over here." Roy stared down at the inky water, now just inches from his face.

At that, the Boxers at the controls wrenched down a lever and the chains flew past, unleashing a shower of sparks and plunging Roy headfirst into the Thames. Wang looked over just in time to see Roy's chained ankles kicking above the surface.

"Roy!" he shouted, spin-turning a brutal kick into the Boxer he was fighting. The man flipped over the side of the barge and into the water. Wang rushed towards the Boxers controlling the crane and took out all three at once with a huge, lightning-fast whirl-kick.

Then Wang grabbed the crank and spun it, lifting Roy out of the water. A sputtering Roy surfaced, spitting water and coughing as his head emerged. "Nasty!" he said.

Just then, another Boxer came out of nowhere, knocking Wang to the deck.

The winch spun.

The chains flew by.

Roy went free-falling back down into the cold, dark river.

Wang leapt up, just in time to duck as a Boxer swung a crowbar at his head. Wang caught the crowbar in his wrist chains and, wrenching it out of the Boxer's grasp, smashed him in the head with the heavy iron object. Then, quickly, Wang wedged the crowbar into his chains and levered it with his body, snapping his hands free.

Wang ran to the winch and cranked away, lifting Roy back out of the water. Just as a spluttering Roy surfaced, another Boxer appeared and began to fight Wang for control of the winch. The two struggled in a mortal tug-of-war.

As Wang and the Boxer fought, Roy was dunked up and down, splashing into and out of the chilly water.

Finally, Wang won control and cranked Roy all the way up to the top of the crane arm.

Roy dangled high above the barge, dripping. "John," he said, "not to rush you or anything, but this is getting old fast."

Wang couldn't answer his friend. A fresh set of Boxers had just appeared in the doorway. Pulling out their swords, they rushed at Wang. Nimbly, he jumped to the top of the wheel, ducking and weaving to avoid their flashing blades.

Then one of those blades sliced right through the cable holding Roy.

With a wail, Roy plunged into the water.

Wang watched in shock, knowing there was no way to pull Roy out now. Then Wang dived and rolled, grabbing the forgotten crowbar from the floor as he cartwheeled through the crowd of Boxers. Crowbar in hand, he jumped over the side to join Roy in the water.

Up on the barge, one of the Boxers scrambled up to the machine gun, locked in an ammo belt, aimed, and began to fire.

Bullets flew over the inky water.

Underneath the surface, in the murky light, Wang used the crowbar to pry off Roy's manacles. Bullets whizzed through the water, making a hailstorm of bubble trails all around them.

When Roy was free, the two friends kicked quickly away from the barge, diving under the door of the dock.

CHAPTER TWENTY:
Artie Has Company

About an hour later, Artie Doyle sat slumped in a leather armchair near the fire, his mouth slightly open as he snored softly. Suddenly he started upright at the sound of a loud knock at the door.

He answered the knock to find Roy and Wang on his doorstep. But they looked — different. Roy wore a trench coat and a plaid deerstalker hat with the earflaps tied up, while Wang was dressed in a tweed jacket and breeches.

"You look ridiculous," Artie blurted.

They pushed past him, into the house. "John," Roy said, "that's the last time I let you pick the clothes." The two of them made themselves comfortable in Artie's armchairs, holding their chilled hands out to the fire.

Artie followed them into the living room. "Every bobby in London is out looking for you two, and here you are on my doorstep!" He showed Roy a newspaper, with sketches of the pair on the front page.

Roy glanced at it and shook his head. "Why do you always get top billing?" he complained to Wang.

Artie grabbed the paper out of Roy's hands. "I really must protest this intrusion," he said.

Wang leaned back in Artie's chair. "Were you sleeping?" he asked.

Artie said sadly, "I might as well sleep. There's nothing else for me to do. My employment's been terminated. That has never actually happened before in my life."

"You were fired?" asked Roy.

"Yes," Artie nodded. "Lord Rathbone saw to that, after I let you escape from his palace."

Wang gave him a sympathetic look. "I am sorry," he said.

Artie shrugged and turned away. Then he made a confession. "Everybody in London's got a novel in their drawer. Here's mine!" He opened the drawer of his huge oaken desk, pulled out a thick wad of papers, and slammed it down in front of Wang.

Curious, Roy checked out the title page. "Fabian Pendergrast, Victorian Detective," he read. He turned to Artie. "Does he kick butt?"

"No," Artie answered solemnly. "He fights for social justice."

"Sounds catchy," Wang said. Then he dropped the sarcasm and got serious. "Artie, we need your help."

Artie stared at him. "Why would I help you two?"

Roy had the answer. "Because Rathbone plans on killing the royal family and taking the throne for himself."

Artie snorted. "Do you have any evidence to support these preposterous allegations?"

Wang pulled out Charlie's dented bowler. "We have this. Use your technique. Tell us where the boy is." Charlie had the Seal. Finding the boy was the first step. If they had the Seal, they could flush out Rathbone.

Artie looked at the bowler. Stammering, he said, "I can't perform on cue! Deductive reasoning takes a clear mind and keen eye. Neither of which I possess at this particular juncture."

Roy grabbed a magnifying glass from a nearby table. "Try this," he said. Then he went to make them all a cup of tea.

They gathered in the kitchen to drink and examine the bowler. Artie stared and stared at it, turning it over in his hands. Finally, he looked up, excitedly. "I have it! Chips of blue-stone and meadow grass! Stonehenge! That's where the boy is."

Wang and Roy sat back in their seats, disappointed. "Slight problem," Roy told Artie. "That wasn't the kid. That was us."

"What in heaven's name were you doing at Stonehenge?" Artie asked.

"We took a wrong turn," Wang told him. "Keep looking."

Once again, Artie examined the hat. He brought it to his nose and took a sniff. "Ah ha! The distinctive aroma of Thames water. The boy is down at the docks."

Roy sighed. "I don't mean to mess up your average, but that was us, too."

Artie tried again. He turned the hat inside out and found some waxy flakes sticking to the lining. He rubbed them between his fingers. "Paraffin wax," he murmured. "Very interesting."

"Maybe the little punk's hiding out in a church," Roy suggested.

"No," Artie mused, "it's not candle wax." Then, suddenly, he sat up straight, his eyes alight. "I've got it!" he cried. "Come on! The game's afoot!"

CHAPTER TWENTY-ONE:
The House of Whacks

Not long afterwards, Artie bent to tinker with the lock on the front door of Madame Tussaud's Wax Museum. Finally, Wang got impatient. Using his Ancient Chinese Wisdom, he picked up a cobblestone and threw it through the window. The three men climbed inside and split up to find Charlie. Not one of them noticed the three Boxers standing in the shadows, watching them.

Artie entered the Ancient Egypt area. He was passing a mural of the pyramids and stepping around a huge wax statue of a camel when he heard something. "Who's there?" he asked, stopping to look around.

A fist slammed into his face, and Artie slumped to the floor.

Meanwhile, Wang stepped into the Chamber of Horrors, where flickering red gaslight cast a strange glimmer over horrific scenes of medieval torture. As Wang glanced around, he suddenly found himself face-to-face with a life-sized statue of the fearsome warrior Genghis Khan. He stepped back with a gasp. Just then, two Boxers stormed towards him.

Wang jumped behind Genghis Khan. As the Boxers approached, Wang saw the figure of Charlie jump out from behind a model guillotine. "Boy! Wait!" Wang shouted. But Charlie slipped away.

The Boxers began slicing the air with their swords, cutting limbs off the statue Wang stood behind. Wang grabbed the arms they'd lopped off and used them to extend his reach, beating the Boxers back.

Their swords sliced at the waxen arms, dicing them into tiny pieces. Wang ducked and wove, avoiding their blows.

Across the museum, Roy strode confidently into the Western Saloon exhibit. It was a classic barroom scene, and Roy felt right at home. Jesse James, dressed just the way Roy used to dress, was busy holding up the bar, brandishing his pearlhandle guns. Roy snorted with derision. "That's *my* look," he muttered. "*I* came up with that."

Suddenly, the saloon doors swung open as Charlie dashed inside. Roy grinned. "You're on my turf now, you little punk," he said, lunging for him. Charlie sprinted away, diving over the counter and disappearing through the mirror on the other side.

Roy paused for a moment to give Jesse James a kick. Then he took off after Charlie. He didn't find the boy on the other side of the mirror, but he did find Artie — lying on top of a waxen Cleopatra.

Back in the Chamber of Horrors, Wang ducked as a statue of an ax-wielding executioner suddenly came to life, swinging his massive weapon downwards. It was another Boxer!

Wang fell back and the axe slammed into the floor just inches from his body. He flipped up onto his feet, snatching a mace from the grip of a waxen Saxon torturer. He whipped the spiked ball on its chain, swinging it into the Boxer's chest.

It disintegrated on impact.

Wax.

Wang looked at it, disgusted. Then, without a moment's hesitation, he spun and kicked, slamming the Boxer backwards into a dungeon. Wang slammed the door shut, then turned to confront the two other Boxers.

They came towards him. Wang springboarded high up into the air to grab the bottom of a hanging cage, and ram-kicked one of the men in the chest. The Boxer fell back into a set of wooden stocks, looking dazed. Before he could get up, Wang kicked open the stocks, pulled out their waxen prisoner, and pushed the Boxer into his place. Clamping the stocks shut as the Boxer slumped forward, Wang spun to see the other Boxer coming at him.

Wham! The Boxer kicked Wang into the guillotine, sending him crashing straight into Marie Antoinette. Her high wig shook as Wang slammed into her. The Boxer reached over to release the shining, razor-sharp blade hanging above Wang's neck.

Wang backflipped away, catching Marie's severed head as the blade sliced through it. He hurled the head at the Boxer, sending him reeling into the torture rack nearby. His weight knocked the turn-wheel so that the wax victim was stretched until he broke in two.

Wang seized the moment to dash out of the Chamber of Horrors.

Meanwhile, Roy made his way down a dimly lit hall. He entered a room, only to come face-to-face with a tall, forbidding figure.

Lord Rathbone.

Roy jumped. Then he looked around. Rathbone was standing very still in the midst of a crowd of people, all wearing crowns. Queen Victoria stood nearby, regal and still.

Statues, every one.

Roy sighed with relief. Then he heard a rustling from under the queen's skirts. Stepping toward the majestic figure, he made a quick apology and bent to rip apart her dress. Cowering between her royal legs was Charlie. Roy grabbed him to pull him out.

Then he noticed the Seal, stuck in the queen's royal garter. He plucked it out and gave Charlie a shove. "Scram, punk, before they ship you off to Australia."

Charlie disappeared. Roy looked down at the glittering Seal, admiring the gigantic diamond. Then he looked up to see Wang and Artie approaching. "Look at that, John," he said, holding up the Seal. "Your old buddy comes through again."

"Thank you," Wang said sincerely.

"Hey," Roy said with a modest shrug. "It's what I do."

Just then, the three men heard a cry. They turned to see a Boxer stepping into view, his shining sword pressed into a very frightened Charlie's neck.

"Give me the Seal," he demanded.

Roy looked over at Wang. He had no choice. He tossed the Seal into the air and the Boxer pushed Charlie aside as he leapt to catch it.

At that moment, the back door of the museum burst open. There was the sound of voices, and the light of many lanterns. The Boxers disappeared. So did Charlie. Wang turned to Roy and Artie. "Come on!" he said. They ran for the front door, storming out into the street.

A crowd of thirty policemen stood waiting for them.

CHAPTER TWENTY-TWO: Captured Once Again

The paddy wagon rumbled over the cobblestone street. High above London, Big Ben loomed, its white face gleaming in the dark, moonless night. It was almost eleven-thirty.

Inside the wagon, Wang stared down at the ivory puzzle box in his hands.

Roy saw that his friend looked depressed. "All right, John," he said. "What's the plan?"

Wang kept staring at the box. "I am out of plans, Roy," he said tonelessly. "I failed my father. Now I have failed my sister."

Roy couldn't believe his ears. "You want to grow old in an English prison?" he asked. "You can't quit now. That would mean Rathbone won!"

Artie stared out the barred window, looking up at Big Ben. "At least we'll have a good view of the fireworks," he said with a sigh.

"Fireworks?" Wang asked, finally looking up from his box.

Artie nodded. "At midnight they're launching a huge display from a flotilla of barges on the Thames. It's the official kickoff to the queen's Jubilee. The royal family will watch the spectacle from a balcony overlooking the river."

Wang looked at Roy.

Roy looked at Wang.

"I don't believe it," said Roy. "Wu Yip has a machine gun on one of those barges."

Wang looked out the window to check Big Ben. "We only have half an hour," he reported.

Roy started shaking the bars that imprisoned them in the wagon. Nothing gave. Suddenly, Charlie's face appeared, upside down!

He was on the roof of the carriage, looking in. "You gents lost your way?" he asked cheekily.

"Charlie!" Wang cried.

"What are you doing here?" Roy asked.

In answer, Charlie held up a ring of keys he'd picked from the pocket of the bobby driving the wagon.

A moment later, four figures rolled out of the back of the wagon. As he dusted himself off, Roy turned to Charlie. "Nice move, kid. Why did you come back?"

Charlie shrugged. "Why did you give up the Seal?"

"I guess I got tired of looking out for number one," Roy said. "Hey, I never did get your name."

"Chaplin," said the boy. "Charlie Chaplin." They looked at each other and shook hands.

Meanwhile, at the Houses of Parliament, where massive Union Jack banners draped the four sides of Big Ben's clock tower, a procession of royal carriages was arriving. A huge crowd watched as uniformed, wigged footmen stepped forward to open the door of the first one. A woman stepped out and the crowd broke into a roar. "God bless the queen!" The shouts rang out as Queen Victoria walked slowly up the red carpet, a trumpet fanfare filling the air. Behind her, the rest of the royal family descended from their carriages and followed her up the carpet.

Lord Rathbone looked calm and elegant in his dress uniform, a scarlet silk sash across one shoulder and his ceremonial saber hanging at his side.

CHAPTER TWENTY-THREE: Ten Minutes to Disaster

Two barges bobbed in the river next to Westminster Bridge, right across from the Houses of Parliament. A thick rope linked them. In the hold of one of them, Chon Lin lay on the floor, bound and gagged. A Boxer stood looking down at her, his face impassive. He looked up as Wu Yip came down the ladder. Wu Yip handed him the dragon-handled dagger. In Chinese, he ordered, *"Once the fireworks start, slit her throat and leave her body by the gun."*

Chon Lin struggled, her eyes wide with fear. But there was no hope of breaking free.

Wu Yip leaned out of the open hatch to check Big Ben. *"You don't have long to wait,"* he told his prisoner.

On the bridge, an excited crowd stood waiting for the fireworks to begin. Pushing through the packed bodies, Artie, Roy, and Wang leaned over the railing and looked down at the barge, thirty feet below. Wang looked up to check Big Ben. Then he turned to his friends. "You warn the royal family," he told them. "I must save Chon Lin."

"But how —" Artie asked, looking down at the barge, far below.

Instead of answering him, Wang swung himself effortlessly onto the railing and somersaulted through the air, touching down softly on the deck of the barge.

"My word," Artie murmured, dumbstruck.

"I know," Roy said. "He's like a human haiku."

Beneath them, Wang padded across the deck of the barge. Like a tightrope walker, he began to tiptoe across the rope tying the two barges together. Then he spotted two Boxers inspecting the fireworks, a last-minute check. He dropped down and finished his journey out of their sight, pulling himself hand over hand along the rope. When he reached the other deck, he pulled himself up and untied the rope. Just then, Wu Yip emerged from the hatch.

Wang watched, hidden in the shadows, as Wu Yip disappeared into a canvas tent set up on the deck.

Suddenly, cheers erupted from across the water. Wang turned to look at the Houses of Parliament as the queen and the royal family fanned out onto the terrace, only a hundred yards away. Wang watched as Rathbone picked a safe position near a stone column that would protect him when the machine gun started to blast away.

A glance at Big Ben told Wang that time was running out. He headed for the hold.

Near the entrance to the Houses of Parliament, Roy and Artie pushed their way through the tightly packed throngs. As they drew closer, they saw that the doors were blocked by at least twenty royal guards standing shoulder to shoulder.

"It's no use," said Artie. "We'll never get past them!"

Roy shook his head. "You gotta get rid of that negative attitude, Artie."

"While I admire your delusionally optimistic viewpoint on life," Artie told him, "at the present you must admit our enterprise looks completely hopeless."

"We've still got one thing they don't have," Roy insisted. "The element of surprise."

"What element of surprise?" asked Artie.

"Me," Roy answered, as he headed for a police horse that was tied up on the other side of the street.

CHAPTER TWENTY-FOUR:
The Clock Strikes Twelve

High on Big Ben's clock face, the two hands came together. Midnight! The gigantic clock began to toll the hour. Below, a deafening roar erupted from the crowds.

On the barge near the bridge, two Boxers holding flaming torches touched them down to light the fireworks. Rockets began shooting into the air, filling the sky with explosions in every color of the rainbow.

Down in the hold, Chon Lin glared up at

the Boxer, her face streaked with tears but still defiant.

Towering above her, the Boxer unsheathed the dagger.

He swept it toward her throat, its glinting blade a dazzling arc.

Out of nowhere, a wooden pulley swung into the back of his head. He crumpled to his knees, falling forward.

Wang scrambled to his sister's side. Taking the dagger from the Boxer's hand, he used it to slice the ropes that bound her. Then he held her tightly. "I am so glad you are alive," he whispered in a choked voice.

Chon Lin pulled free and looked up at him. Then she slapped his face.

"I just saved you!" Wang said, shocked.

"You were late." Chon Lin got up and headed for the hatch. "Come, we must stop Wu Yip."

An exasperated Wang followed her up the ladder.

Outside the Houses of Parliament, all eyes were on the sky. Even the guards were staring upwards, their faces lit by the multicolored rainbow of sparks that decorated the darkness.

Suddenly, there was the sound of clattering hoofs.

The guards looked down, just in time to see Roy galloping into view. Artie was mounted behind him, clinging to Roy's waist for dear life. As the horse drew nearer to the entrance, Roy let out a mighty war whoop. The horse sprang forward, flying high over the heads of the guards and touching down on the other side. Without slowing, it galloped straight into the Houses of Parliament.

Up on the terrace, Rathbone's eyes were *not* on the sky. He looked down, his eyes fixed on the canvas tent aboard the barge. Casually, he strolled to safety behind the stone pillar, just as Big Ben tolled the final chime of midnight.

The queen turned to wave at him. "Nelson, why are you hiding back there?" she called.

"I don't want to impede your view, your highness," he answered, bowing politely.

"Nonsense," her royal self said. "Come sit next to me. You arranged all of this. You should have a front-row view."

Rathbone did not budge from behind his pillar. "I regret that I must respectfully decline, your highness," he said. "I must ensure that nothing goes wrong tonight."

An especially large firework burst overhead, showering the night with a glittering golden spray.

"Nelson," said the queen, "you've outdone yourself."

"Wait until you see the finale," said the elegant Lord Rathbone.

Down on the barge, the two Boxers were bending to light a long row of fuses when Wang and Lin sprang out of the hatch. They did not hesitate as they came at the Boxers, fists and feet flying, fighting in perfect synchronization.

The Boxers did not back down. Flaming torches held high, they fought back hard, landing blow after blow on Wang and Lin.

Brother and sister fought on, beating back the Boxers in a display of harmonized precision. Their hands and feet were a blur of movement, kicking and punching without rest. Finally, they launched into a series of spinning back-kicks.

Wang spun clockwise.

Lin spun counterclockwise.

Both of their kicks landed perfectly, sending the Boxers flying into the pile of fireworks. Rockets and Roman candles exploded in every direction, as Catherine wheels rolled across the deck and star shells flew high into the air.

Wang and Lin made their way towards the tent. Wang ripped the canvas aside, just as Wu Yip locked his sights on the queen and squeezed the trigger of the machine gun. Bullets began to whine over the water.

Wang kicked the barrel of the gun, sending the gunfire strafing far above the balcony that held the royal family.

Up on the terrace, a statue's head exploded. A bottle shattered. A woman's high hairdo burst into flame. Rathbone peeked out from behind his column and peered down at the barge through a spyglass.

On the deck, the machine gun kept firing as it circled around. Its roar was almost drowned out by the booming of the fireworks that still exploded into the night sky.

Chon Lin leapt at Wu Yip.

He snaked out an arm to catch her foot, sending her flying to the deck.

Wang launched himself at his enemy. Wu Yip spun behind him, grabbing him in a choke hold and yanking his head until it was directly in the path of the still-circling machine gun.

Wu Yip smiled to himself as the gunfire crept toward Wang. It came nearer, nearer.

Click. Click. Click.

The clip was empty!

"Duck!" cried Chon Lin just then. Wang turned to see his sister holding a lit mortar in her hands. With Wu Yip distracted for a moment, Wang slipped out of his grasp and spun to kick him to the edge of the barge.

Wu Yip swayed over the side, then found his balance just in time to turn and see Chon Lin still holding the mortar, ready to throw the enormous firework straight at him. He felt for his dagger.

"Looking for this?" Wang asked, holding up the cobra dagger.

Wu Yip glanced over, just as Chon Lin heaved the mortar at his gut. Like a cannonball, the mortar slammed into the emperor's half brother, sending his body flying into the air. He disappeared over the side of the barge, just as another barrage of fireworks lit up the sky.

The crowd cheered. Chon Lin and Wang shared a smile, their faces aglow in the reflected light of a canopy of golden sparks.

CHAPTER TWENTY-FIVE: Rathbone on the Run

"*Yee-haw!*" Roy and Artie galloped down the ornate hallway inside the House of Lords, the medieval portraits lining the walls a total blur as they raced past. They took a corner at top speed, only to see Rathbone coming straight at them.

"*Whoa!*" Roy reined in the horse, blocking Rathbone's way. Artie flew off the back, landing in a heap on the marble floor. Roy gave Rathbone a withering look. "I'm guessing from your hasty retreat that you're still twentieth in line to the throne," he said.

"Tenth," said Rathbone from between gritted teeth.

"After tonight, I'll have a better chance of becoming king of England than you," Roy said with a smile. "Arrest him, Inspector Doyle," he added to Artie, who was just getting to his feet.

"You don't get it, Mr. O' Bannon," said Rathbone. "I'm untouchable. You can't prove a thing."

Roy raised an eyebrow. "I think you're going to have a hard time explaining what you're doing with the Imperial Seal of China," he said.

Rathbone frowned. "For an American, you make a very good point," he admitted.

At that moment, Artie moved in. Rathbone flicked his wrist and the derringer appeared. He fired before Roy even had time to shout "Gun!"

Artie fell to the floor, and Rathbone took off down the hall, unsheathing his ceremonial saber as he ran.

"You okay, buddy?" Roy asked, bending over Artie.

"Oh, yes," Artie managed to gasp. "You don't mind if I faint, do you?" With that, he slumped to the ground. Roy was propping him up against the wall when Wang and Chon Lin ran up.

"We heard a shot!" said Wang.

"Rathbone nailed Artie," Roy explained.

"I'll look after him," Chon Lin said, kneeling at Artie's side. "You two go."

Wang glanced at the crossed rapiers mounted on the wall nearby. He pulled them down and kept one sword for himself, tossing the other to Roy. Then he turned back to Chon Lin. "I will avenge our father," he told his sister.

"I know," she answered, meeting his eyes. Then she turned to Roy. Suddenly shy, he turned away, but Chon Lin pulled him into an embrace. "Be careful," she said.

CHAPTER TWENTY-SIX:
Hickory, Dickory, Dock

Following Rathbone, Wang and Roy burst through a door only to find themselves staring at a steep spiral staircase. *Pow!* Rathbone fired from above, missing them by a mile. They heard a muffled curse, and then the empty pistol rattled to the ground. Wang and Roy began to climb.

Soon they found themselves at the very top of the tower, deep inside the huge, complex cogs and gears of Big Ben's clock. Hanging catwalks crisscrossed the space between the clockworks, and the four glass faces of the clock glowed in the moonlight, their hands and numbers making strange shadow patterns on the inside of the tower.

"Show your face!" Wang cried, as he and Roy stormed into the area.

Silence.

Roy headed up one of the ladders and began to cross the catwalk, warning an unseen Rathbone of his skills as a swordsman. Suddenly, out of the shadows, Rathbone leapt onto Roy, snatching his sword away and kicking him off the catwalk.

Crash! Roy's body went flying right through the glass clock face. *"Aaahhhhh!"* he cried, as he disappeared.

"Roy!" Wang shouted after him.

There was no answer, except for Rathbone's evil laugh. Wang watched, hatred etching his features, as Rathbone flipped Roy's sword up so that he held two weapons. Wang grabbed a rope and cut one end so that he could swing over to the catwalk where Rathbone stood. "You killed my father," he said, stepping nearer to the lord, "you killed my friend. Now I will kill you." He sliced his sword at the tall, elegant figure.

Rathbone parried the blow and thrust another in return, and the two stepped along the catwalk, blades flashing and clanging furiously. Suddenly, Wang cried out in pain as a line of red appeared across his arm. Enraged, he slashed back at Rathbone, ripping his jacket.

The Imperial Seal tumbled free and rolled across the slats of the catwalk. Wang lunged for it and managed to catch it just before it rolled off the edge. In the process, he dropped his sword. It clattered into the cogs below.

Wang crouched, defenseless beneath the towering lord.

Rathbone smiled. "Give my regards to your father," he said, swinging his sword for the final blow.

As the sword flashed near his throat, Wang arched backwards. The sword sliced through the line of support ropes that held up the catwalk. Rathbone looked stunned as the other ropes began to snap and the catwalk collapsed, catapulting both men into the same clock face Roy had already smashed through.

They shot out in an explosion of shattered glass. Then gravity took over.

They began to fall.

CHAPTER TWENTY-SEVEN: In the Nick of Time

It was a long way down, but before he fell even a few feet, Wang felt a hand grab his wrist.

It was Roy, clinging to the hour hand of Big Ben.

Rathbone plunged downward as Wang stared at his friend.

"Cheerio, guv," Roy said, smiling.

"I thought you were dead!" Wang said in disbelief.

"Please, John," Roy said, "it's going to take

more than a tea-drinking psycho to take out Roy O' Bannon."

While the two talked, Wang's fallen sword wedged itself further and further into the inner cogs of Big Ben's works. Inside the tower, sparks flew as the entire network of cogs suddenly froze in place. Bolts began to pop and cables began to snap.

The hour hand swung straight downward, nearly throwing Roy off the clock face. Wang, clinging to the minute hand, managed to hold on while Roy grabbed on to his belt.

The two of them looked down. The ground lay far beneath them.

"John," Roy said, "I'm open to suggestions."

Wang stared at the Union Jack banner flapping beneath them. "We jump," he said.

Roy gulped. "I was kind of looking for something less suicidal."

"Aim for the banner," Wang told him.

Roy took a breath and looked at his friend. "John, I just want you to know, you're the best sidekick I ever had."

"Thanks, Roy," said Wang. "I feel the same way about you." He looked down again, then back at his friend.

"On three," they said together.

Together they counted.

"One."

"Two."

"Three."

Neither of them let go.

"You said 'on three,'" Roy said.

"So did you," Wang reminded him.

They counted again.

"One."

"Two."

"Three."

They let go, screaming at the top of their lungs as they dropped down to grab hold of the banner. They held on tight as the fabric ripped, plunging them downwards on the middle part of the banner. As they came to the bottom of the banner, their newly ripped bungee cord of fabric flew them out, away from the tower.

They were still screaming as they plunged through the roof of a carriage and crashed to a stop on a plush red velvet seat.

They blinked, realizing that they were still alive.

Then they heard a cough.

Wang turned to see whose carriage they had invaded, and saw Her Royal Highness herself, Queen Victoria.

He waved. "Howdy," he said.

The Queen eyed the two men curiously. "Howdy," she echoed.

CHAPTER TWENTY-EIGHT: Rub-a-Dub-Dub

"In recognition of outstanding bravery," said the queen, as she tapped a kneeling Wang on the shoulder with the blade of her sword, "I dub you Sir John Wayne."

She stepped over to Roy and tapped the sword on his shoulder. "For outstanding valor, I dub you Sir Roy O' Bannon."

Next, she turned to Artie, whose head was bowed and whose arm was in a sling. "And for steadfast dedication to justice, I dub you

Sir Arthur Conan Doyle," she said, tapping his shoulder lightly with the sword.

At that, Artie began to sob.

The queen stepped back. "Arise," she told her three newest knights.

They turned to face the crowd. Wang grinned at Chon Lin, who stood in the front row beaming back at him.

Later, as they stood outside Buckingham Palace, Wang carefully placed the Imperial Seal into a box Artie held open.

Chon Lin watched. "Father would be very proud of you," she told her brother.

"No," Wang corrected her. "He would be very proud of *us*."

A carriage rolled up, and Lin climbed inside.

Roy joined Artie and Wang. "So, Artie," he asked. "Does this mean Scotland Yard is welcoming you back with open arms?"

"My official crime-fighting days are over," Artie told him. "The queen has asked me to accompany the Seal back to China. The voyage will give me time to work on my latest novel. It's about a new detective. He has a sidekick and an evil nemesis, and he is going to solve crime with deductive reasoning."

Roy nodded approvingly. "What's his name?"

"Actually, I was going to call him Sherlock Holmes, if that's all right with you," Artie said.

Smiling, Roy gave him his blessings. "Word of advice," he added. "Give him a lady friend this time." He waved as Artie headed off. Then he turned to Wang, who was trying once more to open his ivory puzzle box.

"That was very kind of you, Roy," said Wang.

"Please," Roy said. "Sherlock Holmes? That's a terrible name for a detective." He watched Wang tinker with the box until he couldn't stand it another second. "Come on, let me stomp on it and get it over with," he said, trying to grab it out of Wang's hands.

They pulled back and forth at the box.

Suddenly, it clicked open.

They stared at it, stunned.

Then Roy reached in and pulled out a small, smooth black stone. One side was engraved with gold Chinese letters.

Wang took it from him and translated.

"Family is forever, my son. I am proud you cast your own stone."

Wang and Roy looked at each other. "That's beautiful, John," Roy said. He paused for half a second. "Now, about your sister . . ."

Wang looked at him. Then he smiled and nodded. "Go."

Roy smiled back. Then he went over to the carriage where Lin was waiting. "Now that I'm a Knight of the Round Table," he said to her, "I was wondering if you wanted to get together sometime. Maybe come to America and hang out?"

"Sure," Chon Lin said, smiling down at him. "But no more fights."

Roy thought about it for a moment. "Sure," he said. "I can live with that." He climbed into the carriage next to her, beaming. Leaning out to call to Wang, he said, "We're going to be a family, John! The House of O' Bannon will prevail!"

Wang smiled wearily. Then he climbed into the carriage with his sister and his friend. As the carriage took off through the courtyard, a row of soldiers snapped to attention, saluting the heroes. Wang and Roy waved back.

As they pulled up to the train station a little later, Roy turned to Wang. "John, I've got a business proposition for you."

Wang looked alarmed. "No more zeppelins," he said.

"No, no, this is way better. Moving pictures. Movies, for short. It's all happening in California. You could be a big star! All that Kung Fu stuff you do. What do you say?"

Wang considered. "John Wayne, movie star," he said. "It could work."

Unseen by them as they unloaded their baggage, a familiar face popped up out of one of the big trunks. Charlie. A mischievous smile lit his face as he pulled down his bowler. He'd wiped a dirty hand across his nose, leaving a mark that looked like a black mustache. He lowered himself back into the trunk that was about to cross an ocean. That face was about to become familiar to generations of moviegoers.

As the friends strolled to their train, Roy was still musing about the movies. "I've already lined up our first project," he told Wang. "It's a screen adaptation of *Roy O'Bannon Versus the Mummy*. And the best part is, I can play Roy O' Bannon, and you can play the Mummy."

Some things never change.